Former
Virgin
Short Fiction

Former
Virgin
Short Fiction

by

Cris Mazza

Normal

Published by FC2 with support given by the English
Department Unit for Contemporary Literature of Illinois
State University and the Illinois Arts Council

Address all inquiries to: FC2, Unit for Contemporary
Literature, Campus Box 4241, Illinois State University,
Normal, IL 61790-4241

Former Virgin
Cris Mazza

ISBN: Paper: 1-57366-033-7

Produced and printed in the United States of America

Cover art & design: Todd Bushman
Book design: David Dean

ACKNOWLEDGMENTS MADE TO THE FOLLOWING PUBLICATIONS IN WHICH THESE STORIES FIRST APPEARED:

Mid-American Review and Love's Shadow (Crossing Press) for "The Cram-It-In Method"

Nebraska Review for "Let's Play Doctor"

North Dakota Review for "Adrenalin" and "The Career"

Breaking Up Is Hard To Do (Crossing Press) for "Adrenalin"

American Letters & Commentary and Net Books and Forbidden (Alyson Publications) for "Dog & Girlfriend"

Aethlon: The Journal of Sports Literature for "Caught"

The MacGuffin for "The Dog Doesn't Care and the Woman's Too Sleepy"

Crosscurrents for "Coptorport on Cowell's Mountain"

The Los Angeles Times Magazine for "Bad Luck With Cats"

Black Ice for "Laying Off the Secretary"

Kansas Quarterly for "The Something Bad"

Chicago Review and Fiction International for "Hesitation"

Beloit Fiction Journal for "Former Virgin"

Former Virgin
Short Fiction

The Cram-It-In Method

Maybe Annie's father never taught her (like mine drilled into my head) that force doesn't make anything work easier. This morning I had to refold all her grocery bags because she doesn't flatten them along the seam so they'll stand upright between the refrigerator and cabinet. She tries to smash them in there without folding first—the cram-it-in method. Also the trash can was overflowing, a deluxe pizza box wedged in and a coke bottle balancing on top of that. She could've emptied the trash and started over instead of just pushing in more than it can hold.

I guess I've been living with her for almost a year, but I've managed to never see her. She answered my ad for a roommate and we settled the details by phone. I told her to feel free to go about her usual business. I certainly never wanted to be a witness to anything. Don't I have my own problems to worry about? I stayed in my room when she moved in. I'm in my room whenever she's home. I'll be here when she leaves in her white dress and veil. She wasn't engaged when she moved in, just a college girl in her final year, with (I thought) no worries farther ahead than Saturday night's lover. I didn't know—when she moved her stereo and four speakers, double bed and television into the apartment; nor when I first saw her make-up remover, three kinds of shampoo, tampons and minipads, and her diaphragm kit (which she sometimes leaves on the sink shelf, and I have to see it there, then it disappears again), I didn't know then (and never wanted to know) that Annie was going to have an even bigger problem than her yeast infection (which she treated with yogurt, marked *not for eating* in the refrigerator, and which some of the boys she screwed mistook for a social disease and were angry about—one guy with sensitive skin actually caught it). Maybe I saw it coming when she pointed out so someone on the phone,

What can anyone do with a sociology degree, especially if I don't go to graduate school, which my parents want me to, but I don't. I'd rather take time off from school for a while ... but still, what can I do—? My parents, of course, would also like to see me married, which I wouldn't mind, but there's no one to marry. All of a sudden I seem to know less boys now than ever, (just Mick every other Saturday, but that'll never amount to anything). It's scary—what if I don't meet someone this year?

When she studies, she does it in the living room or kitchen. She keeps a mail order catalogue on the coffee table with her school books, and one night while reading, she took a break to order some underwear with lace. She always washes them by hand and leaves them hanging to dry in the bathroom where I have to see them. SCARY. I thought it was funny how she used that word. No, I never meant FUNNY.

A few months ago I was in the living room when I heard her key in the lock, so I went to my bedroom before she came in. She had a low voice with her. After making sure they weren't talking about me, I didn't really listen. They giggled a while and they turned the stereo on, then some silence, except an ad on the radio for control-top panty hose, interrupted by talking and a few more giggles, on and off—put my teeth on edge, the giggling, but thought I was handling it, covered my head with a pillow—then they went into the bedroom, bounced on the bed a few moments, and they left the apartment together. I came out to use the toilet. I shivered in the bathroom and noticed the soggy condom I didn't want to see in the trash can, half-hidden among crumpled tissues.

Later that night she called a friend,

Let me tell you what happened today, something that only happens on television, I was walking to a class and this guy was waiting outside the building, watching girls—you can always tell when a guy is watching girls—so when I went by he said something like "Hi cutie," or something, then he walked me to my class, and when class was over, I came out and he was waiting for me and he walked me to the next class, and after that class he was there again, waiting for me, I was going home then, so he walked me home, and we got talking. Listen to this, he's good-looking. Well, his hair's real short, but that won't be forever `cause right now he's in ROTC and National Guard Reserve, and as soon as he serves four years as an officer after graduation, he'll be out and can let his hair grow. The army pays him, though, and also he gets social security `cause his mother died when he was little. Anyway, he stayed and we talked and horsed around a little—we danced and I stood on his feet, then we rough-housed on the living room floor. He's strong too, he works out. Huh? ... Oh, his name's Zack. But this is the part that's really weird, listen: We got carried away, after he kissed me a few times, and we wrestled around, we almost did it in the living room, but we made it to the bedroom, and he was a virgin! That's right. Well, he seemed to know what to do, technically he seemed to know, then afterwards he told me he'd never really gone all the way before, but he must've known something `cause he was fast! It was over in two minutes, I swear, not more than two minutes. I didn't say anything this time, I could tell he didn't want me to be the leader, he's in the ROTC. Then he gave me his dogtags—no one's done that to me since high school rings. It's sort of sweet, you know? I guess I'll play along with him, it's been a long time, since I dumped Roger in the 10th grade, remember that? ... Okay, he dumped me, if you want to get technical. What? ... Yeah, maybe he just needs experience. He calls me the all-American girl and says he's the all-American boy. But he noticed my tummy and says I have a little pot, and he was poking it. I like my tummy, he embarrassed me .... Anyway, he wants us to be the all-American boy and girl. I guess I'm going to have a boyfriend for a while.

She called all her friends, in order of importance. The story got shorter every time, but she never forgot to tell the parts about his virginity and the ROTC. Sometimes one amazed her more than the other, then vice versa on the next call.

Three weeks or a month later she went through the whole phone list again to tell them all she was engaged.

> *We're telling my relatives we've known each other for five or six months .... Probably in June, Then he'll be an officer in the army. Oh—Julie's doing the engagement party, and I think Carol has the shower. I'll probably have a shower with my mother's friends too.*
>
> *Yes, you'll be a bridesmaid.*

That's when the cards started coming, and Annie tapes them to the outside of her bedroom door where I have to see them too. Most of them are silhouettes of people in a sunset, a few close-ups of hands holding each other. One card is a couple of gold rings on a little pillow next to two glasses of pink champagne.

❏

This is Friday evening and Zack has gone to a military fraternity meeting after being here all afternoon, locked with Annie in her dank bedroom. (I've gone in there a few times when she's not home—only to look for the dictionary which she uses as padding between the bed and the wall, otherwise she causes all that banging when she screws because the headboard slaps the wall between our bedrooms. As it is, the dictionary usually slips free halfway through. Her bedroom smells of stale clothes and not-often changed sheets and is damp because she keeps a pan of water on the radiator.) Whoever's on the other end of the phone is being updated.

- Zack's still too fast and I don't know how to tell him without hurting his ego.
- I figured out he thinks it's more macho to be fast like that.
- But really, how can you tell someone they aren't doing sex right ...
- No, I'm not getting anything out of it. I'm not sure he knows that I'm supposed to ...
- Yeah, I'll have to tell him somehow. I've still got my books from my human sexuality class—I'll put them on the night stand.
- The other thing is now that he's tried it without a rubber, he likes it better that way.
- Huh? ...
- I'd get another abortion ...
- It's not his decision to make ....
- Yeah, he'll have to realize that if he doesn't want to wear one, at least I've got to know in advance so I can get prepared ...
- Yeah, I decided on six bridesmaids.

   In the morning Zack is here again. I can hear his voice through the wall, so I use the toilet quickly before they come out of the bedroom. But they talk a long time in there today, then the bed creaks pretty steadily. She must have the dictionary—the headboard isn't knocking on the wall. Voices again, mostly hers, like the sound of a Morse code telegraph machine. I keep hearing the same strings of dots and dashes, I can't understand her—don't want to understand her.

   When they do come out, they go into the kitchen and I wouldn't be able to hear them if Annie wasn't half screaming. **MY PARENTS WILL HAVE TO TAKE OUT A LOAN FOR A BIG WEDDING! LISTEN: I WANT A SMALL, SIMPLE CEREMONY, MAYBE A HUNDRED TO A HUNDRED-FIFTY COUPLES, A**

BAND, LIQUOR, A SMALL SUPPER, SIX BRIDESMAIDS, SIX USHERS .... I DON'T CARE IF IT'S FREE, I DON'T WANT A MILITARY WEDDING. I'M THE ONE GETTING MARRIED, I GET TO PLAN IT, IT CAN BE JUST AS NICE IF IT'S SMALL .... I'M THE BRIDE AND THE BRIDE MAKES THE PLANS. LISTEN: A BAND, A HUNDRED-FIFTY, TWO-HUNDRED COUPLES— IT'LL BE PLENTY, THE LIQUOR ALONE WILL COST A COUPLE THOUSAND DOLLARS, MY PARENTS'LL PROBABLY ASK YOUR FATHER TO PAY PART OF IT .... WHY NOT, YOU'RE GETTING MARRIED TOO. YOU'RE SUPPOSED TO PAY FOR THE FLOWERS AND BOOZE AT LEAST, THAT'S IN ALL THE BOOKS, BUT LISTEN: A COUPLE-HUNDRED COUPLES, A BAND, WE'LL FIND A HALL, THAT'LL BE PLENTY BIG ENOUGH, WE DON'T NEED IT ANY BIGGER.

After they're gone, I go out to eat and find their broken egg shells and the empty tub of real butter, and there, forced into the loaded trashcan, is the milk carton that was almost full yesterday. She always pours the milk down the drain on the morning of the date that's stamped on the carton. On the table is a copy of *Modern Bride*, the spring issue, all the brides in white, every single one of them.

❑

If I'm already asleep I don't hear them come in at night until the headboard starts banging the wall. I needed the dictionary today. Sometimes the headboard pounds like a heartbeat, then it goes back to a single downbeat, or sometimes it misses a beat. But no voices at all, not even loud breathing. It's like hammering nails, a carpenter on the job all night, his work never finished.

I can hear cartoons on the tube while Annie's in the kitchen frying something. I smell butter. She yells *breakfast* twice, and at the end of a cartoon the TV goes off and they're both in the kitchen. He eats in five minutes then goes out to a morning class and she heads for the telephone. The floors creak, different pitches in different parts of the room. The boards near the phone always groan when she picks up the receiver.

You'll never believe it ...

No, worse ...

I told him, then we read about it together.

I didn't want to just come out and say he stinks in bed!

It's hard to hide the fact that I know more about sex than he does.

I can't help it, I took a class.

But he pretends everything I know is from that class, not from experience,

so I'm careful to never say, when this happened to me before,

or, I know a guy who does this or that.

I have to say I read it somewhere ...

yeah, well, he seemed to understand, but—huh? ...

No, just the opposite! Now he can't finish...

No, I can tell when I take my diaphragm out that he didn't ... Actually no, it's not much fun because that's all he worries about—he says he has to make it in order to prove he loves me, so that's all he's trying to do, and, well, the harder he tries ... exactly, I showed him in the book, but—huh? ...

Well, yeah, but I don't want to be his goddamn sex therapist!

When I return the dictionary later, I spot the sex manual on the nightstand, not opened. I flip through it, but she hasn't highlighted nor underlined anything. One of the positions is called female-superior ... her on top, doesn't look like it would make much noise. There are some dead plants in her room, but the bed is made and the dirty clothes are all piled on one chair. A fishnet is mounted on the wall over the bed as a decoration.

When she comes home, she takes the phone to the kitchen, so I shouldn't have to hear too much. But the longer she talks, the faster; and faster always makes louder. So by the time the usual greetings are over, I can hear every word.

Well, it's a big mess, listen:
His father wants to give us some money, right?
He's been saving it for Zack since Zack was little.

but his father wants us to put it away
or let him invest it for us for a nestegg.

My parents want Zack's father to pay
for half the wedding, but I'm afraid if he does that,
that's where the money'll go.

Which is why
he doesn't want to help pay for the wedding
because he wants us to invest the money
so when Zack is out of the army
we'll have something put away.

Anyway, I want to use some of it for the honeymoon—
I decided on the Virgin Islands,
and we can get a couple of weeks there easy
for what he planned to give us—
they sent a brochure and I've already decided on it,
I'm making reservations.

His father doesn't know yet,
and tomorrow we're all having dinner together—
my parents are planning to ask him
to pay for half the wedding,
especially since Zack's the one who wants it big.

but I've already told him
two-hundred fifty couples tops,
a hundred fifty will be mine and he gets a hundred
—we made our lists—
so I told him not to meet any more people this term
because we won't be able to invite them
and they'll wonder why.

He wanted to wait until some people said
they couldn't come and then send out more invitations
to fill the empty places, but I said no,
the invitations are sent once,
maybe a month or six weeks ahead of the date,
then no more go out, so don't meet any more people,
I told him, we can't afford it.

I can smell macaroni-n-cheese. When she goes back out for her afternoon classes, she leaves the pan on the stove, half full of yellow-orange noodles. I put the stuff into a freezer container, I can tell there's real butter in it. Then I wash the dishes from this morning. Looks like eggs again. Zack uses a lot of ketchup on his. She's left a few new magazines here. In the *Bridebook* I find a questionnaire, already filled out, *How long have you known the groom-to-be? Where do you intend to live? Do you already own stainless cookware? What type of honeymoon?* It's a multiple-choice test. *How much will your wedding dress cost?* She checked the middle choice, between one and two thousand dollars. *Who will do the cooking? Who will manage the budget and pay the bills? What kind of literature have you found most helpful in planning your new life?*

On the phone late Sunday morning, she says she has to do some studying and write a paper. She's found a dress, she says, which she wants all the bridesmaids to look at in Macy's, it's only $500.

Well, I recognize what phase he's in, I went through it
too—but I was in high school, you know, when I first did
it... Now he'sgoing through that phase—you know, he
wants to experiment. It's only fair, I guess, to let him
have his turn, but really, I got over all that, but you
know he reads about something and he wants to try it...
I remember when I was doing that, because everything
was new, but now it's only new to him, Well, I go
along with it because it's
only fair...

When he gets here, they have strong-smelling fish for dinner, then they leave the kitchen and go into her bedroom. They turn the stereo on to try to hide their noises, but they end up drowning out the music. Like two carpenters not hitting their nails at the same time. Then one carpenter finishes his nail and the other is left banging all alone. When that one stops there's just the music, but they turn that off too, and there's silence, until Annie starts talking. I'm pretty sure she's not talking about me. Her voice goes faster and faster, shriller and higher, and I can't understand any words. She has plenty to say, or if she forgets where she is, she starts over. Then she screeches, *I HATE YOU*, and something thumps like a butt on the floor or a head against the door, and her voice starts again, jabbering, a record on the wrong speed. His voice is there too—he's not taking this lying down—but his voice is a weird high falsetto, a breathless cartoon voice. The next thing I can understand is when she screams *GET OUTTA HERE*, and more thumping. But the door doesn't open and no one creaks footsteps on the living room floorboards. I've lost track of time. One of the carpenters starts hammering again, so the other shuts up.

She doesn't get to make any more calls until the next afternoon when Zack leaves for close-order drill. She says,

Hi. Ready for the latest? You know, his mother's dead and all. Well, Saturday night he takes me into his father's attic and gets out this trunk ... yeah, like a horror movie. And he pulls out this dress wrapped in plastic and mothballs and holds it up. His mother's wedding dress, see ... it was okay, nothing great, it might've once been white, high neck and sleeves to the wrist. Then last night he tells me he wants me to wear it when we get married. He said it's the way he always pictured his wedding. I told him it won't save any money because we'd have to have it tailored to fit me, and cleaned and pressed, and somehow get rid of the mothball smell. Yeah, well, I didn't make any promises.

She sleeps most of the day until her father arrives to take her home for a family supper. Later she comes back to the apartment howling, walking around crying—not hitting anything or stomping or throwing anything, but she cries like an ambulance. Not sorrow, but absolute terror. When Zack comes in—he has his own key—the siren stops without a grumble. Maybe she was singing, it could've been singing. I can hear her showing him vacation brochures.

> **LOOK AT THIS—THIS IS THE ONE I'VE CHOSEN, VIRGIN ISLANDS, SEE, YOU GET**
> - **A PRIVATE BUNGALOW**
> - **SAUNA**
> - **MEALS INCLUDED**
> - **THERE'S A POOL AND**
> - **BOATS AND**
> - **THE ROOMS ARE MODERN AND AIR-CONDITIONED,**
> - **FULLY STAFFED AND PRIVATE.**
> **I'LL MAKE RESERVATIONS.**

When I use the toilet after they go to bed, I find his shaving gear piled on the sink shelf. I take my toothbrush and soap back to my room.

It's not until Friday that she finally has time to call her bridesmaids again.

Yeah, for another two-hundred down we could've gotten a later time in a different hall. Anyway ... no, he doesn't care, know what he's been doing? Listen, we get along together and start fooling around, then he says, Let's play teacher and student, and he makes me pretend I'm his student and he's a teacher, and he's teaching me how to do it, and I'm supposed to pretend I never have and he's showing me. I have to say stuff like, Oh, is that where it goes?, and say eeek when I see it ... well, if it'll help....

I have to go to the bathroom!

I can't hear as well from here, but I notice she washed her control-top panty hose and hung them on the towel rod where I have to see them. By the time I come out, she already has another bridesmaid on the phone.

> Well, at least with the earlier time we won't have to rush to the airport. We'll have all afternoon to get ready and relax. You know, the ceremony will probably be exhausting for both of us.

> Yeah, we're going to need those two weeks alone together.

> Not exactly, but today he wanted to play two kids experimenting, so we had to pretend we didn't know anything about it and were finding out about it together, like we're both surprised when it gets big, all that stuff. I don't know.

> Yeah, I ordered those dresses at Macy's.

When I finally have a chance to come out of my room, I can't find the dictionary, so I look through her pile of schoolbooks on the coffee table. No dictionary, but in *House Beautiful* magazine there's an article on solutions to age-old room-divider problems, and here's another little magazine, *Handbook of Creative Lifestyle*, a marker in the chapter called daddy-and-mommy, but the mommy wears spike heels and fishnet stockings and a gunbelt with bullets, breasts disguised as gold-tipped missiles, and the daddy sucks a bullet-shaped pacifier. Why did I have to see this?

❏

Can't really say I'm on the outside looking in. It *is* our living room window—four windows up, two over—but I can't see inside. The drapes are closed. I call from the corner drugstore in a booth with no door and snow underfoot. She answers after one ring—half a ring, and she's already on the line, eager, breathless ....

Who is this?

It sounds so different to hear her *through* the phone. Last time she spoke on the phone—this morning, to her mother, she screamed and stamped her feet, then lowered her voice and

talked quickly, almost a hissing whisper, almost positive I
heard my name.

Hello? Hello? Anyone there?

It's been a long time since she's said anything was SCARY. I can't
remember what her voice sounded like when she said it. Not any
louder or faster or less intense. Just more like a real voice.

**HELLO? I KNOW YOU'RE THERE,
I HEAR YOU BREATHING.**

Is that a laugh? She's laughed before, but not like this—brittle
and metallic and thin. Hard to listen to, makes my ear feel
frozen to the receiver which will have to be ripped away, leaving
my head bleeding.

**ROGER, IS THAT YOU, YOU WEIRDO?
YOU GOT THE WEDDING ANNOUNCEMENT I SENT,
DIDN'T YOU?**

If she looked out the window, she might see me at the phone
booth, not that there'd be any new flicker of recognition in
her voice. What difference would it make if she did?

*I know it's you, Roger.
Zack wanted to send the announcement,
as a joke,
he asked who my last real boyfriend had been.
What's a matter, it make you jealous?*

Lots of other times I couldn't understand every word like this.

❏

I just noticed the milk carton has tomorrow's date, February 15,
the expiration date. I'll pour it out and save her the trouble. But
the phone is ringing and I'm about to answer it the same time
she comes in the door. I get back to my room just in time, still
holding onto the half-full milk carton. She's alone.

Cris Mazza

Just got in. What? Oh, Zack's all upset 'cause his father wants to move out but Zack doesn't want his father to sell the house. He grew up there. Huh? No, I can't, I'm going into the city to price some rings .... Well, he was going to come too, but he has National Guard duty,

> *and then tonight*
> *he shows me this little ring box*
> *with his parents' wedding rings and he says he wants to use*
> *them.*
> *He said his dad said it's okay.*
> *His father hasn't worn his in years,*
> *and Zack says he would like me to have his mother's wedding*
> *ring ....*
> *No, it was kind of plain. I didn't try it on.*
> *I sort of want my own, you know, braided gold, a wider band,*
> *maybe*
> *something set in it, something special ....*

I said we've got a while to decide. Want to come with me tomorrow? ... Wait, Zack's at the door. What's he doing here? Anyway, I'll speak to you tomorrow.

Her bedroom door squeaks and their voices mumble together in there. The bedsprings whine and the headboard rattles against the wall, and their voices mumble again. They may be talking about me. But they finish talking before I can hear, and the bed bounces and the headboard knocks and very soon, very soon Annie breathes eagerly. I can hear her little voice in every breath, on the verge of a sneeze.... Then something crashes, and the headboard rat-a-tats out of rhythm, and Annie's voice is oh-oh-oh-oh, higherandhigher. No sound from Zack, no grunting, just his carpenter noises and her piercing scream, screaming and screaming, the headboard like a machine gun now, and Annie screaming like the scene of a crime, but I plug my ears with my fingers and I think I'm crying ... or maybe it's her crying (at last) and I'm the one (finally) screaming my head off.

Let's Play Doctor

The nurse shaves away her pubic hair.

"I wonder if Joey will like this." Dee props herself up on her elbows and watches. The nurse doesn't use shaving cream or water, and yet it doesn't hurt. "Looks like a baby," Dee says, and laughs.

Then she has to stand on the floor and bend over across the examination table while the nurse shaves between her buttocks, holding the sides apart with two fingers. She must be a good nurse—not a single nick, scratch or drop of blood.

"I guess you'll be lying on your side for a while," the nurse says.

"Yes, a double-whammy!" Dee is seemingly unable to say anything without the breathless half-laugh. She's just repeating what Dr. Shea said last week when he decided to remove the cyst near her tailbone after he repairs her hernia.

"You know, neither the hernia nor the cyst has ever bothered me, never any pain or anything. They seemed to bother Joey more than me. He was afraid he was going to hurt me or something."

"You don't look old enough to be married." The razor makes a scratchy sound.

"Looks can be deceiving, you know," Dee says. "We've been married three years."

"Just about time for another honeymoon."

The nurse stops shaving for a second as Dee giggles. "We never had a real honeymoon."

"Never too late to start."

"I'll tell him," Dee laughs again.

"Hold still, okay?" The nurse holds her buttocks farther apart, the razor moving intricately around Dee's anus. "You realize you won't be able to, or shouldn't try to have intercourse for at least three weeks."

"Oh, I know that. Joey knows too."

She'd asked Dr. Shea last week in the final pre-surgery exam. He'd probed the hernia gently, then she rolled over and he touched the cyst, lying just under the surface, and he'd explained the procedure, then tapped her bottom and told her to get dressed.

"What about sex?" she'd said. Joey never told her to ask.

"I'm afraid you'll have to wait a few weeks, after the surgery. Tell Joey I'm sorry." Dr. Shea is as thin as a young tree, and when he smiles he's *all* smile.

"That's okay," Dee said. "He doesn't care. I mean, it's no big deal. He's not worried about it. I mean, it's not as though it's going to change anything. Is it?"

"Won't make a bit of difference." Dr. Shea began lowering the examination table, with Dee still on it, lying on her side, wearing light blue underwear and a paper examination gown. She'd shaved her legs that morning, had taken a shower and sprayed a little deodorant in her crotch. He kept his hand on her hip while he lowered the table. A nurse was in the room, holding Dee's chart.

"It's no big deal," Dee repeated.

Another nurse comes in to put silly paper slippers on Dee's feet and a blue paper poncho over her head. "We're ready for you." The three of them walk to the operating room and Dee climbs on the table.

"Dr. Shea's still at the hospital, but the anesthesiologist is here," says a third nurse, already masked. The three nurses turn their backs and begin to scrub. Dee can hear their voices under the running water. Whoever they're talking about had to be reminded about something over and over and everyone's beginning to wonder if she'll ever get it right and how many chances is Dr. Shea going to give her before he—But maybe she's providing him with other services. *Him?* Well, why'd he hire her then? *Him?* The three nurses laugh. Dee turns her head and smiles at the big man who comes in and introduces himself, but she can't understand his name through his mask. He attaches some round things to her chest so everyone in the room can hear her heart beat. She keeps one eye on the door, but Dr. Shea doesn't arrive before the other doctor has already attached an IV and shoots something into the tube so the drowsiness begins like an eclipse.

Then she can hear Dr. Shea's high-pitched voice and the nurses mumbling. One of the nurses says, "What's ten inches long and white? Have you heard this one already?"

"Nothing," Dee says. She can't see anything because the paper poncho is pulled up over her head.

"Is she awake?"

"Hi, Dee!" Dr. Shea says.

"So what's the punch line?" a nurse asks.

"That's it. What she said."

"You knew that joke, Dee?" Dr. Shea says. "Okay release it," he says, in a different voice.

"I remember another joke," Dee says with a chuckle. "But it's too nasty. You know what? I can't feel you doing anything."

"I'm almost done. Go ahead, tell your joke."

"You sure? Okay. How do you make a hillbilly girl pregnant?"

"I don't know. How?"

Cris Mazza

"Come on her shoes and let the flies do the rest."

One nurse groans. Dr. Shea says, "What? I didn't catch it."

"Don't make me repeat it, it's awful, isn't it? Come on her shoes and let the flies do the rest. You can change the hillbilly to anything—Italian, Mexican, whatever—but I use hillbilly cause I'm from Kentucky, so no one can say I'm making fun of anyone else ...." She closes her eyes. She can't feel him touching her. Not like last week. He has very soft hands and long fingers, well-manicured and without heavy calluses. Of course he does, he's a surgeon.

"Did Joey tell you those jokes?" Dr. Shea asks.

"Joey? No, I never tell him nasty jokes. I get 'em from a book ... in the library, that is, I go to the library every night while Joey's at work."

"I gotta get me that book," a nurse says.

"Very hard to find. Not all libraries ...."

The bookstore is a block *past* the library, in between a cult movie theater and a health food store. A bakery and coffee shop inside the bookstore—where apparently people are allowed to sit at tables and read new magazines—seem to make the store warmer than most. It's a fairly small bookstore, but has a whole wall of magazines, organized by sexual preference. Dee always walks past them, slowly, back and forth, but hasn't yet ever taken one and sat at a table with a tempting croissant. Of course the joke book is on the humor shelf and she reads a few jokes every time—but not at one of the tables—and when the smell of the baked goods gets too overpowering, she leaves. The air outside seems to be shockingly cool—sometimes she gasps.

She wakes puking as they wheel her back to an empty examination room. A nurse walks beside her holding a little dish to catch the vomit. She can't hear Dr. Shea and can't move to look for him. The gurney is narrow and she's on her side. They tell her not to roll one way or the other. She continues puking. Joey

26

arrives to take her home, but she's still puking and can't leave, so he sits beside her all afternoon, holding her hand and reading *Sports Illustrated* while she pukes. There's probably poetry in that somewhere.

Eventually she's home. She heard Dr. Shea giving Joey some instructions. He said she could have a bath on Saturday. Joey drove carefully, but she puked once on the way home anyway. She sat on the edge of the bed, doubled over, then fell sideways, curled in a ball on her side, noticed the bouquet of carnations Joey had put on the night stand, then closed her eyes and the nausea began to fade. Dr. Shea had told Joey that if she didn't calm down tonight, call his service and they would get in touch with him. She reaches blindly to the night stand to make sure the plastic vomit bowl is close at hand. Joey comes in to say he has to go to work. He sits on the side of the bed and strokes her head.

"Touch my places," she says. "The scars."

"I don't think that would be a good idea."

"Okay, it doesn't matter." She moves one hand, slowly, from where it was tucked between her thighs and pushes it under her pillow, beneath her head. "You won't have to call the doctor tonight."

He pulls the sheet over her shoulders. It's an early summer evening. When he's gone, she opens her eyes once more. The carnations are white and pink, but look gray in the twilight. She was a virgin when she met him.

It might be later, but not too much later. She seems to be watching herself as she gets out of bed, not appearing to need any help, apparently not weak or sore. She brushes her long hair, seeing herself—she might be in the bathroom looking in the mirror, but she can see the *back* of her head, the brush swishing through her hair which hangs to her butt. Her hair was blond when she was younger, even when she got her drivers license. It's been light brown for several years but looks blond again now. She breaks off one of the carnations and puts it behind her ear. The flower is some bright, exotic color, but she can't really tell what color it is. Her reflection seems to be coming from a wall of glass, like a picture window. She leans close, shading her eyes to help herself see through. Apparently she already left the house, locked up, walked briskly down the sidewalk, as she does every evening after Joey goes to work. If she passed the library, she didn't recognize it, and the bookstore has changed too—she can't see any books through the window. In fact, she can't see through the window. It's black, huge and opaque, and all she can see is herself trying to look through.

"Aren't we going to go inside?"

The voice doesn't startle her. It's Dr. Shea. He's with her. Either they came together or he met her here. He looks too young to be a doctor, especially in his green scrub suit which makes his neck look longer and his smile even more toothy. "Show me where you learned your jokes."

Suddenly she's hot, burning up, and presses both hands to her face. "It's okay," he says. "From now on *I'll* teach you all your jokes." He takes her hand.

The bookstore is extremely hot and humid. It's like a heavy coat hanging on her shoulders. The heat seems thick around her and she paddles with her free hand, passing thousands of racks of books, looking for the wall where the magazines are. "I know they're here somewhere," she says. Even though it's so oppressively hot, she's not sweating. But when they find the magazines, they walk back and forth because she doesn't recognize any of them. "This isn't right, where are they?" It doesn't even seem like she's searching for the magazines. She's looking at his hand holding hers, as though she's still standing behind herself. He strokes her knuckles with his thumb.

"Don't you want to look at one of them?" he asks,

"Yes, of course."

"You don't need to be afraid. We'll say it's doctor's orders."

She has a magazine in her hands and Dr. Shea moves behind her, very close, his cheek against hers. The smells from the bakery at the back of the bookstore become potent. She sees a whole pan of buttery cinnamon rolls coming out of the oven. She doesn't let go of the magazine; she can feel the slick heavy pages in her hands. Dr. Shea kisses her neck. "Let's check your wounds," he murmurs. She's looking at the magazine but doesn't see anything. Dr. Shea lifts her shirt and runs his finger along the line where he had cut her open. She had bandages on when she got home from the hospital, but they're gone now. She can see the place, a red line where the two flaps of her skin are sewn together with invisible thread, his finger moving back and forth across it. She shudders. "Did I make you do that?" he says. She must be mute. Or there's nothing more to say. She can see him smiling, like maybe she's watching from a different angle now, but she's still holding the magazine and he's digging his finger between the stitches then pushing it inside. She doubles over, pressing her butt into him, and he seems to bend over around her. The magazine could be a mirror or maybe she's looking out of the pages, watching herself and Dr. Shea, but sometimes she can't tell which one is her. She's never moved her hips like that. His hand moves into her gently, cupping each organ in his fingertips. He's a surgeon so he'd know if something was wrong with her.

"Now the other place," he says, turning her around. He holds her buttocks and rubs the wound on her tailbone with his thumb. There's blood on the front of his scrub suit. Bread is baking. The hot odor of it makes her dizzy for a minute. Then he turns her sideways and maybe holds her with his knees, his chin over her head, but his legs and arms and neck are just warm places pressing against her, and the room is so hot anyway it seems hard to tell if it's really him—except for his hands. Each of his hands is on one of her wounds, reaching inside, feeling the slippery pieces of her. She's wiggling and arching her back, but he doesn't tell her to be still. Every once in a while she can feel the magazine in her hand. She smells the bread baking and looks at the blood on his shirt. She asks if it's hers without having to say anything. "You started your period during the surgery," he says. His hands are pushing harder, farther, his fingers spread, softly touching everything they find, although her heart is too far away, and his hands aren't reaching that direction. She must have her eyes closed because she can't see anything anymore, not until his hands meet each other in the middle. He must be clasping his hands together, making a gentle fist that seems to throb, matching the sound of an uncontrolled heartbeat coming from somewhere else, which everyone in the bookstore must be able to hear. She can see her own mouth open and her entire body arch, her head thrown back and she is alone, writhing and moving freely through the pea-soup heat, holding a heavy magazine. Her arm is tired. It's dark and somehow she got back to her bed before Joey came home. She can hear his key in the front door and she can see her hand lying on the mattress beside her, the weight of the magazine tingling in her palm, a pounding soreness in her guts, underneath the bandages. He comes in to ask if there's anything she needs. The room is freezing and she begins to sob but doesn't answer him.

The Career

Ten years before they ever met in a motel room, Kevin and Dolly first came upon each other in Dolly's brother's loft bedroom where Kevin was being tutored in high school algebra. Dolly couldn't understand anything they were talking about. She interrupted to ask a few questions before her brother shooed her out. She was almost eight. Two years after that Kevin would marry Margie, although he didn't know it at the time. Meanwhile Dolly's brother went away to college and later became a pilot. He left his yearbooks behind.

Dolly never bought any yearbooks of her own. She wasn't in any of the photos of clubs or teams, and nobody had taken a picture of her writing on the restroom walls, which is what she spent a good deal of time doing, when she wasn't visiting various stalls to see if anyone had responded to her messages. She was heavy from the time she was a baby—a chubby child, a fat teenager—until without warning, when she was 17, she grew a few inches and slimmed down dramatically. Around that same time she moved her bed—just her bed—out of her small ground-floor room and found a place for it in the attic, near a small window which she kept open for ventilation. It never measured up to her brother's bedroom—an upper floor addition with a separate entry up a flight of outdoor stairs. Instead of giving his loft to Dolly, her parents moved into it after her brother moved on.

She was almost 18 the evening of the 10-year reunion for her brother's graduation class. Kevin stopped on his way to the

Cris Mazza

party to see Dolly's brother, but by that time Dolly was the only one home, wearing cut-off shorts and a loose white tank top, no bra, barefoot, and her nose was peeling. She had been slicing a watermelon and came to the door still holding the knife, a few seeds stuck to the blade. She offered him a piece but he said he had to go—Margie was waiting in the car. Less than an hour later, Kevin called from the party and told Dolly where to meet him the next day.

Dolly was supposed to be going to summer school in order to graduate, but she told them she had a job interview and had to leave class early. She picked up a sandwich on the way to meet Kevin at the TreeTop Inn, and while she sat on the edge of the bed eating, she told him how the school had changed since he and her brother went there. "We didn't even have a prom," she said, licking her fingers. "Everyone was too busy being friendless, outcast and unloved to get dressed up for a dance." She wiped her hands on the sheets. "You knew my brother, didn't you?"

"Of course."

"Did you see him at the party last night? He's a fighter pilot now." She wiggled out of her clothes. Kevin only had an hour for lunch. "But wait a minute," Dolly said. "There's something you should know."

"What now?"

She laughed, bouncing on the bed. "Well, I used to look at my brother's yearbooks, and I named everyone, you know, like Goofy, Greaser, Hippy-boy ... but you were the easiest to name, you and my brother. I thought you should finally know. I named you Handsome. Jeez, I can hardly believe my brother was the same age in that picture as all those terrible boys I went to school with."

Kevin flipped her onto her stomach and told her to get on her knees but keep her shoulders and face down on the bed. "I always wanted to try this, but Margie doesn't—"

"Doesn't what?"

"Just doesn't. Now knock off the gab."

"Yes sir." She laughed, her voice muffled in the sheets.

If he'd asked, she would've said it felt nice. Then she might've told him about the time her father was watching an ERA rally on the news and said, "What is it you women want, anyway," so she had thought about it in the attic, flipping through yearbooks, trying to decide, and maybe this was it, but not just because it felt nice. But he didn't ask.

He zipped his fly, picked up her underwear and tossed them to her.

"You know what?" she said. He was combing his hair, using the polished surface of the vanity desk as a mirror. Then he finished and continued leaning over the desk, staring down at the reflection. "I think you really needed this," she said. He didn't move. "Don't worry," she went on, "I won't be asking you to get divorced. That's not what's important to me."

"Oh. You'll want money." He still didn't move.

"No!"

"Then what do *you* expect to get out of it?" He finally turned. His eyes were vivid green, his face unusually pale.

"You act as though I've got something *planned*," Dolly laughed. "Like I've been preparing for this with a list of demands to negotiate." Kevin adjusted his belt and brushed lint from his pants. "Kevin, believe me, I hardly *ever* have anything planned." She stopped to inspect a scratch on her shoulder. "You know my brother also asked me what I want—when he was home for the reunion, he asked me what I want to do, and I didn't even have an answer for *him*. You know, I'm proud of my brother, I really am, and I'm *not* jealous that he's the apple of my father's eye and I don't *wish* I was NASA's secret weapon."

Kevin checked his watch, then wound it.

"Maybe *this* is all I want," she said, and he looked at her again, quickly. "Or something that this could be, with a little work. *I'm* willing." She finally picked up her underwear and began putting them on. "Well? Say something!"

He stared for a moment more, then said, "I'll be calling you—during the day. Don't tie up the phone."

She smiled and finished dressing when he was gone, then

went back to school and dropped her summer school classes.

Very quickly they had a twice-a-week routine. There were enough cheap motels that they could go three months at a time without repeating one. And there were almost as many positions in bed. Kevin complained about the cost of the motels, but Dolly laughed. "As soon as you get a job, we split 50-50, okay?" he said. That's what was so funny.

"I don't have time for a job!" she gasped, trying to keep a straight face.

Dolly studied sex manuals and did several sets of exercises every day to stay in shape. Sometimes Kevin would collapse on his back, his face ashen, his eyes pale and watery, his hair slick with sweat, and he would groan, "Oh my God, you little slut!" That made her smile too.

"I should write an article for *Reader's Digest* that marriage isn't so tough, like they always say it is," she said.

"What the hell do *you* know about it?"

"I'm doing the same work!"

"You know, every time you open your mouth you set a new record."

Dolly laughed.

For a few years it stayed that way, only the positions changed. Dolly no longer needed to study sex manuals, so she began reading her mother's women's magazines. Articles like *How Women-Who-Work Work on Their Marriages*, or *How To Tell If You're Important to Him*, or *Decorate Your Bedroom With Bedroom Eyes*.

"I've been thinking," she said.

"You mean you've been reading pulp magazines again."

Dolly laughed. "No. Well, yes, but this is different. I mean, I don't even know where you work."

"That's right."

"Well, for all I know you're a vice officer."

"So what?"

She laughed again. "I also don't know what your hobbies are. What do you do all day Saturday and Sunday?"

"What difference does it make?"

"I thought maybe we should have some similar interests."

He wrote the name of the next motel they would use on a scrap of paper and tossed it toward her.

The next evening Dolly knocked on Kevin's kitchen door.

2

Dolly had never seen Kevin in blue jeans before. The kitchen smelled like spaghetti sauce, but there were no dirty dishes anywhere and Kevin was holding a dishtowel. He just stood there, staring, holding the door open, even after Margie joined them in the kitchen. Dolly said, "I'm a friend of Kevin's."

"Well, come in. I'm Margie." She had thin blond hair in a pony tail, a thin face with pale gray eyes, and lots of freckles. The three of them stood looking at each other. Then Margie said, "Excuse me for a second. I have to get my laundry in the dryer."

Dolly turned grinning to Kevin as Margie left the room. "So that's why you wanted me."

"Shut up. What the hell are you doing here?"

"Improving our relationship."

A baby cried somewhere in another room. "You have a kid!" Dolly said. "And you never even told me it was born or anything!"

"Why should I tell you?"

"Don't you think we should know each other better by now?"

Kevin was already on his way to see to the crying baby. He turned and said, "I want you gone when I get back." But by the time Kevin finished with the kid, Margie and Dolly had set up a scrabble game on the kitchen table. Nobody did very well— none of the words was over four letters. The kid kept Margie busy. Once when she was out changing a diaper, Dolly leaned close to Kevin and began licking the inside of his ear. Later that evening he saw her out to her car and screwed her quickly on the back seat before returning to the house.

So Dolly got her way and they began spending one or two evenings a month together, playing 3-handed card games or Monopoly, and smoking dope. Margie always got sleepy first. "I don't want to get you in trouble, Dolly, isn't it getting late?"

"You're forgetting," Kevin said, "Dolly doesn't have any reason to get up early." His face was tan except a white mask around his eyes where his sunglasses usually were. "Or to get up at all," he added. Dolly laughed.

"What are you going to do, Dolly?" Margie asked.

"You mean when I grow up?" She grinned and put her hand in Kevin's crotch under the table.

"I mean as a career or something," Margie said.

"Gosh, I can't decide between being a sex-therapist or a factory worker." She gave Kevin a squeeze. He was staring at the cards as he shuffled them. "But then I start imagining life as a factory worker. There you are, sweaty, out-of-shape, ugly, ten hours a day pasting labels on tuna cans as they pass on a belt, then going home and taking a nap in a room with big brown stains on the walls, then staying up as late as you can in the night—watching old movies on a fuzzy black-and-white television with a busted speaker so there's no sound—because as soon as you go to bed you'll have to wake up and paste labels on tuna cans again, every day until you're dead." She paused. "No one can be dumbly content *all* the time—like an animal with a full stomach or a race horse put out for stud."

"Why not?" Kevin said.

Dolly still had her hand in his crotch. "Whose turn is it," she asked.

Gradually Dolly began arriving at their house earlier and sat with them in the kitchen while they finished eating. The baby had grown into a kid of two or three and spent his time showing off how well he could throw food on the floor or blow mouthfuls across the table. Kevin ignored him when he got that way, but Margie snapped, "Stop it, Lance," and slapped his hands. "Kevin, why don't you make him behave," Margie said while she wiped the kid's screaming mouth with a damp rag.

"Why me?"

"I'm always doing it—now he thinks I'm some sort of ogre so he runs to you for protection."

"God you're paranoid."

The kid finally stopped crying and was staring with glossy eyes at Kevin. "Whew," Dolly said, "you guys must have strong ears." After Margie returned from putting the kid in his bedroom, Dolly went to the drawer where she knew they kept the cards, in with the knives and forks.

"So what do you think, Kevin," Margie asked, "should we send Lance to nursery school in the fall?"

Dolly sat beside Kevin at the table, slipped her sandals off and slid her bare feet up Kevin's pant leg.

"Why do I always have to make all the decisions?" he said.

"You're the one who earns the money," Margie answered, smiling a little. "That makes you the boss."

"That's bullshit and you know it."

"Did you say something to me?" Dolly asked. She was polishing a ring with a paper napkin, then put the ring back onto her middle finger.

"Anyway, I do make decisions, Kevin," Margie said. "Every day I'm making decisions but you don't seem to notice them."

"Don't give me that crap."

Margie sat down. "Let's talk about it later, Kevin."

"Okay," Dolly said. "What game shall I deal out?"

"It's up to Kevin," Margie said softly.

"I know," Dolly laughed. "He holds our very fate in his hands." Again Margie smiled slightly, but Kevin didn't.

When the kid was around 5, Margie flew east for an uncle's funeral. Dolly told Kevin it would be like a vacation for her if she could stay in his bedroom.

"A vacation from what?" he said. But he let her stay one night, and he said if she came out of the bedroom he'd throw her out of the house.

She didn't have much to do while Kevin was out having

supper with the kid, playing with him and reading stories until the kid went to sleep. She dug around in some drawers and discovered a vibrator, but it didn't have any batteries. Kevin also had some men's magazines which she looked at while she waited for him. He didn't come in until after 11, but he got undressed right away and got between her legs.

"Hey." She tapped his shoulder with the vibrator. "How come you never use this on me?"

"You don't need it." He was thrusting so hard she had to drop the vibrator and hold onto the sides of the mattress.

"Is that supposed to be an insult?" she said, laughing.

"Suit yourself."

"Then I'll take it as a compliment."

Afterward she flipped through one of the magazines. "I know what I could do," she said. "Why couldn't I be a model for these magazines? If I hadn't dropped out of that photography class in high school I could've taken my own pictures and sent them in."

"You're really hopeless."

"I've got a lot of hope!" Dolly laughed.

3

"I think we're ready," Dolly told Kevin.

He stopped buttoning his pants and stared at her. "What're you talking about—we just finished."

"Not that." Dolly got off the motel bed, pulled the bedspread and sheets down and got in. Sometimes she slept an hour or two after he left. "I mean," she said, "we need to get together someplace else. Come to my place for the weekend. My parents are on another trip. They're visiting my brother, I think."

"Are you out of your mind?"

"Bring Margie and the kid—I don't mind. They've never been a problem. We're friends aren't we?"

Kevin sort of laughed and got out his motel directory to choose the next place. "Forget it."

"Why, Kevin?"

"You sound like Lance, *why daddy why?*"

"Well—*why?*"

"Let's just leave well enough alone." He wrote on a scrap of paper and put it in her purse.

"Come on, Kevin, is well enough really *good* enough?" He was already going out the door.

That night, after a game of hearts, while they smoked some dope, she described her parents' house to Margie. Of course Kevin had already been there, years before. All the walls were natural wood and there was a round fireplace in the middle of the large front room—living room furniture on one side, the dining table on the other. The kitchen also was in the front room—in a corner, separated only by an L-shaped counter. The only other rooms were her small bedless bedroom where she exercised, and her parents' old room which had become the television room. In between those was the door to the attic. And of course there was her brother's—now parent's—loft bedroom with its own bathroom and private stairway access from the garden on the side of the house. "It's like a tree house. A private miniature little house. You can have it when you visit."

"I didn't know you had a brother," Margie said.

"I still do. He's very important to the military somehow. Isn't that the ultimate success?"

"The military?"

"No, not *that*, but you know, they'd give him a raise and promotion if he was going to quit. They'd give him a civilian job with all sorts of benefits if it kept them from losing him."

"You're talking about job security," Margie said.

"No, not just that either. He's *important* to them."

Then Margie said, "What do you think, Kevin?" He shrugged, pursed his lips and blew out some smoke, so Margie accepted the invitation. Dolly said this weekend was her 28th birthday.

Dolly made a lasagna for dinner, but the sauce boiled over while she was exercising. She didn't have another can of tomato puree, so she had to open some Ragu, and it tasted funny. Then she shaved—legs, armpits, everything—and put on her white bikini. They were all meeting at the beach.

Margie wore a huge hat and sunglasses and had white sunscreen smeared all over herself. Her lips seemed thinner and pale, and she looked more skinny and more freckly. She was irritable when she spoke to Lance. He was 8 and ran around kicking up sand, splashing and collecting seaweed.

"Just think, Kevin," Dolly said. "When you first saw me I was like Lance." Kevin sat squinting toward the water. Margie lay on her back with her hat over her face. If it wasn't for Lance, no one would've talked. Kevin sent Lance to go pee in the waves, then he stuck his finger inside the leg of Dolly's bathing suit, but he didn't smile. He was also wearing sunglasses, the mirror kind. He took his finger out before the kid came back. The kid poured a handful of sand on Kevin's arm, then brushed it off, but the fool's gold stayed on his skin and sparkled. Kevin plowed into the sand with the finger he'd used in her bathing suit.

Everyone was hungry so they didn't stay long at the beach. As soon as they walked in the house, before Margie even looked around, she told Lance not to touch anything. Kevin stood in the middle of the room but didn't say anything, not even to Lance who was asking what he could do. Dolly got the lasagna out of the refrigerator and started the oven. Then Margie noticed that her lighter was missing.

"You don't smoke, do you?" Dolly asked.

"Oh, Kevin," Margie moaned. She emptied her purse on the L-shaped counter. "I couldn't have lost it at the beach, could I?"

"I'll get you another," Kevin said.

"I don't want another!" Margie stopped looking through her things and stared at him. He stared back. "Well?" she said.

"I don't know what's wrong with you, Margie," Kevin said, then started examining the books in the wall-long, ceiling-high bookcase.

"Kevin, please!"

Dolly stood leaning with her back against the kitchen sink, arms folded. "What's that for?" Kevin asked her.

"Huh?"

"That dirty look. C'mon, Dolly, spill it."

"Kevin, please," Margie repeated. She threw her empty purse onto the counter beside her pile of stuff. "Doesn't it mean anything to you?"

"It must've cost all of two ninety-eight."

"I don't care!" Margie's eyes were wet and her cheeks splotched pink. "You gave it to me!" She started to cry, quietly.

"Okay, okay," Kevin shouted. "I'll go back and look for it." Then he stopped on his way out the door and turned toward Dolly. "You're going to tell me about that dirty look later."

After Kevin's car screeched out of the driveway, Dolly took their suitcase and led Margie out through the glass slider, around the corner of the house, through the garden, then up the secluded staircase into the loft. Margie's eyes brimmed again as she looked around. The late sun outside the only window made the whole room rosy. There were fresh flowers on the night stand and dozens of candles of all sizes. Margie turned and hugged Dolly. "Oh, Dolly, things haven't been going well. We really need this." Dolly smoothed a wrinkle on the bed. "Thank you for doing this for us," Margie said, wiping her eyes and smiling.

"It's okay," Dolly murmured. "I know what you mean."

They were in the front room, not really talking—Margie flipping through a *Scientific American* magazine and Dolly taking an armload of salad vegetables out of the refrigerator—when Kevin returned. Margie leaped over the coffee table to hug him, and she said something, but her voice was muffled and trembling. Kevin looked over Margie's head at Dolly. "Supper ready yet?" He was patting Margie's back and still had his sunglasses on.

The kid came in talking about something he was doing. Kevin said he would come out later and see whatever it was, but

Margie grabbed the kid's wrist and took him to the bathroom. Dolly picked up all the salad vegetables and dropped them back into the refrigerator. She went to check the lasagna, but she couldn't open the oven because Kevin had stepped close behind her and was pressing her up against the door.

"Now, tell me about that dirty look," he said. She yelped, pushed him backwards with her butt, then faced him, an oven mitt on each hand. "It was a *smile*, wasn't it? Your little spats are so cute," she laughed. "But I don't know whose side to take."

Kevin backed up. "Listen, baby, those fights are just plain stupid, like your mouth."

Dolly pretended to spar, grinning, using the oven mitts like boxing gloves, dancing around him. "Don't call me baby, buster."

"I have a few other names for you too."

"Like what?"

"Slut."

She suddenly noticed he hadn't taken his sunglasses off yet. She could see a small version of herself in each lens, and she watched herself laugh. "I've heard that before."

He began unbuckling his belt. "I'm going to show you something. You think you've seen a *fight*?" He unzipped his fly, opened his pants and pushed his underwear down a little. "Look at that." He was running his finger through the hair. Dolly bent close and saw a white scar.

"Looks like an appendix scar," she said. "My brother had one."

"Shows how much you know." Kevin zipped and buckled his pants, went into the front room and picked up the *Scientific American*. The kid ran in and jumped on Kevin's lap; Margie flopped into a chair. "I swear, Kevin, he makes me so exhausted." Kevin wrestled the kid over to the table, put him in a chair, tickled him, and told him not to be a slob. When Dolly explained about the sauce, Kevin agreed that the lasagna tasted funny. But Margie thought it was wonderful.

"Maybe I'll be a chef," Dolly said, licking cheese from the

serving knife. "Or open my own Italian restaurant."

"You could do anything you wanted to, Dolly, once you set your mind to it," Margie said.

"I know," Dolly said. "Did you ever have a job?"

"I was a loan officer for five years."

"Wow. Why'd you quit?"

"A lot of reasons. Lance was born. And I had some trouble there. One of the other officers kept harassing me .... you know what I mean."

"Getting on your case?"

Kevin rolled his eyes and shook his head. Then he suddenly leaned across the table, pointing at Dolly. "*There*, I saw that, that one was a dirty look!"

"You're crazy. I was smiling again."

"I mean harassing me by flirting," Margie said. "You know, touching me and teasing me in front of the tellers about running away with him to Mexico, stuff like that."

"He liked her freckles," Kevin added.

Margie put her fork down. "What's that supposed to mean?"

"Nothing. I was kidding."

"I can't help it if I have freckles, Kevin. I tried hiding them with make-up, but you didn't like that either."

"Hey—I said I was kidding! For God's sake, Margie!"

The kid was staring. "Lance, you're excused," Margie said in a tight voice. Her face was red again.

"I'll be out in a minute to see your fort," Kevin called after him.

Margie sat tapping her knife in her plate. Kevin leaned back in his chair and stared at his feet while Dolly cleared away the dishes. She squirted too much soap in the sink and ran the water. Margie came to the kitchen counter and took a cigarette from her purse. "I'm supposed to be quitting," she said.

"All these years, I never saw you smoke before. I didn't think you did."

"I keep quitting on and off."

Kevin put his sunglasses on and went outside. Then it was quiet and Dolly could hear the suds hissing. She plunged both hands down into the sink and found she'd only run a few inches of water underneath the pile of suds. She almost cut herself on the knife she'd used to serve the lasagna.

"Maybe I could get a job as a dishwasher," Dolly said softly. She soaked her hands in the warm water while Margie finished her cigarette. Then they both went outside and found Kevin sitting on the lawn. The kid wasn't around. Margie sat beside Kevin, leaning on him, and didn't ask where the kid was. Kevin had rolled a joint for the three of them to share. They smoked it in silence, watching the sun go down, listening to the mocking-birds and the shouts of kids somewhere playing street baseball. A few mosquitoes zinged past their ears. Dolly tried to get silly, but Kevin said she was forcing.

"I don't think this stuff is any good," Margie said.

"It's working fine for me," Kevin answered.

The kid came running around the corner of the house so Kevin hid the joint under his hand on the lawn. The kid kneeled, looked around at all three of them and sniffed the air like a dog. Kevin stared at the kid, then said, "What's up, pardner?"

"What's up with you?" the kid said.

"We're just sitting here like boring adults. Why doncha go find something more exciting to do."

"Will you come with me?"

"It's bedtime, Lance," Margie said.

"But it's still light!"

Margie sighed, gave Kevin a look, then walked to the back door. The kid cried, but followed Margie into the house.

"Poor Margie," Dolly said.

"Yeah." Kevin had to re-light the joint, holding it with a pin. He sucked hard and handed the pin to Dolly. "So," he said, "tell me about those dirty looks you've been giving me."

"I haven't been."

"Liar."

Dolly looked at him. There wasn't a single gray hair hidden

in the blond, and no lines on his face. She knew under the sunglasses his eyes were greener than bottle glass. "You gonna tell me?" he said.

Dolly smashed the rest of the joint into the grass under her heel. "You never tell *me* anything. What was that scar from, anyway?" Kevin shook his head and looked away. "Maybe I'll become a marriage counselor," Dolly said. She crawled closer to him. He was sitting with his heels digging into the lawn, his arms wrapped around his knees. Dolly unbuttoned his shirt and slid her hand down his chest to his belt buckle. She squeezed her fingers under his waistband, but he suddenly turned, pushed her to her back and sat on top of her, pinning her wrists to the grass above her head, She wiggled and laughed without making any sound. Kevin ground his pelvis against hers. "See—" Dolly giggled. "You don't need to get divorced, Kevin. You still have me. At least I've never held a knife on you to get you in bed with *me*, right?"

Kevin's hands tightened on her wrists, then he released her and stood up. His shirt was hanging open. It was almost dark but he still had his sunglasses on. He said, "You really know how to ruin everything."

She tried to get up but couldn't move. "Are you still holding me down?"

"More and more often I can't stand you. You're so incredibly stupid." His voice was soft and tight and he spit a little, but she didn't feel it fall on her. "No wonder you're such a failure."

"I'm not." She thought she was laughing, but that's not what it sounded like.

"What have you ever succeeded at?"

She had to concentrate and strain to raise her foot and touch his leg. She tried to hold onto his pants with her toes. "I'm important to you," she whispered.

"Think again, baby." He backed up and her foot fell heavily to the lawn. "God, out of the sack you're tedious. Maybe you could have a great career as a piece of ass, but I doubt anyone could put up with you as long as I have. I can't believe you and

●

your brother are even remotely related."

The sky was a beautiful deep blue with just a few pinprick stars. Mourning dove were still calling and night bugs were screaming. She could feel every blade of grass which was touching her arms and legs. Again it seemed too difficult to move, but she managed to roll over. She pulled her knees under herself and tried to crawl away. Her arms felt like rubber bands.

"No you don't," Kevin whispered. He grabbed her ankle and her elbows buckled. Her chin hit the grass.

"Let go." She kicked her leg. "Let go, let go."

"Shut up," he hissed.

"Let go!" She sat up and hit him in the jaw. He grabbed her wrist in his other hand. "Let go, you bastard!"

"Shut up, Dolly, I'm not kidding."

"Let go, let go, let go!" She tried to kick him in the face with her free foot, but he sat on her leg, then lunged forward and pinned her to the ground again, sitting on her stomach. This time he didn't hold her wrists. He put his hands around her throat. "Shut up, I'm serious, shut your mouth!" He bounced her head on the lawn. Her teeth snapped together and she bit her tongue.

"Are you going to keep quiet now?"

Dolly stared up at him without blinking.

"Okay." His hands softened on her neck and he stroked her gently with his fingertips. "Now you be a good girl and I'll take care of you later." He stood and brushed off his pants as Margie came out of the house. She went to Kevin and buttoned his shirt. "I swear," Margie said, "I'm ready for a whole one all to myself." She took Kevin's sunglasses off. "Will you roll it for me?"

"I thought you said the stuff wasn't working for you."

"Oh you know how I am," Margie said. Dolly rolled over and hid her face in the crook of her elbow.

"What's wrong, Dolly?" Margie asked.

"She's stoned," Kevin said, "and she's going to bed, right Dolly?"

"Leave her alone, she's not a two-year-old."

"Could've fooled me."

"Stop being ugly, Kevin," Margie said. Dolly got up and began walking toward the house. "He didn't mean it," Margie called. "It's this dope. I'm going to throw this batch away."

"Yeah, I'll come apologize later when it wears off," Kevin said.

Dolly watched her reflection approaching in the sliding glass door and stopped short just before she hit the glass, when she was face-to-face with herself. She stared, then went into the house and directly to the attic to her bed.

There were a million crickets outside, and frogs, and some night birds, and dogs barking, and she heard one cat fight. She was sweating and her arms and legs ached, but she didn't stretch or move. She heard a car start outside. The engine roared and backfired a few times, then tires squealed as the vehicle drove away. The words to a song repeated over and over in her mind, and the melody didn't seem to have a proper ending but just kept starting again. She wondered if she was hearing a radio from the loft. Another car started and car doors slammed. There were voices in the street outside, but she couldn't understand what they were saying. She tried to cry but found herself counting seconds as her watch ticked in her ear, then she lost track of how many times she reached sixty. She was afraid to look at her watch because it might say it was only nine-fifteen, or it might say six and the sun would be up soon and she hadn't moved all night and might never move again. Then the door creaked open, and someone whispered, "Dolly?"

She rolled over so fast she put a kink in her neck. "Who's there ... who is it!"

He ran into a box of books—the sex manuals—and cursed, then turned on the light. "I've been looking all over the goddamn house for you. Why is there no bed in your *bed*room?"

"What do you want!"

"What do you think."

"No!"

He slammed the door. "If you think you can just quit on me, you're dumber than I thought."

She jumped out of bed, still dressed in shorts and shirt and sandals. She thought he was holding something—a stick or flashlight or knife—but when he hit her there was nothing in his hand. It felt funny to cry. It didn't feel like laughing.

"Come on, Dolly," Kevin said, chuckling a little. "We've been together ten years."

Then he came toward her again, but she turned and made it out the window before he reached her. She may have even flown for a while before she fell.

Dog & Girlfriend

She is trained to stay off the bed. Somehow she understands this rule to mean only her back end. She's perfectly capable of keeping her little feet on the floor and taking a nap with the rest of her body on the bed. She also uses this position, when I'm in bed, to ask for things. So she gets up there, puts her head on the blankets, two silly feet still on the floor, and says she wants to die. She thinks she's pregnant again.

But I'm hardly in a position to respond. She didn't say I'm *ready* to die. She's just mad, so I'm letting her cool off which proves she didn't mean it. I'm still busy after being tubed.

Familiar position. Isn't it? How much other trouble will it cause? He would only touch me with his cock. He wouldn't mind getting *it* dirty. I never had that talk with my mother about freshness. I scratch down there in my sleep. It takes a long time, but I shave the whole shebang, nose to toes.

What if I'd told my girlfriend it was her father? My girlfriend might've said, What do you think you're doing, trying to take my mother's place so then you can say *come back to the womb*? Clever girlfriend.

I'm treating myself for yeast infection. Staying inert on the bed long after ejaculating the medication.

How'd you get the man, she wanted to know. Dressed like a female impersonator, let him get tanked, then said my sex change operation was in progress, wasn't complete, getting a hairy chest, but no cock yet.

I finally get out of bed, take the leash off the hook by the back door and my dog says she's ready to chase squirrels. Maybe she forgot what she told me while I was on my back. Dogs don't remember, unless the incident in question is accompanied by a traumatic occurrence or great reward, putting into her memory: *repeat this*, or: *don't*. Which I don't think happened. Sure, the medicine is white like semen, but when I say, *you want puppies?* she looks into the trees shouting for the squirrels to come down and face off.

She's wrong, I wouldn't say *come back to the womb*, even if fucking someone who could've been her father might make me somehow her mother. If she hadn't left, I'd say, I don't want you in my womb, I don't want anyone in my womb. But you let *him* go *part* way in, my dog says, that's more than *I* did. She's still proud of that. She refused the stud and had to be artificially inseminated.

So, is the hair on my body repulsive? Thick, stiff and black, armpits, crotch, legs. That's par. Then I hit 30 and it's coming in on my chin and upper lip. On the big knuckles on my big toes. A ring around each nipple. Next it'll be sprouting from my earlobes. But my girlfriend shouldn't've said, yeah, some dykes like hairy women, but not *me*. Maybe it was her first time being a girlfriend as well as being a first girlfriend. My dog wanted to hump the stud. We're a fine pair.

Every time I came out of the bathroom, I shouted, Where are you! I'd been hiding it. I got the depilatory system down pat. Then the top of my head started going thin. So I figure, what's the use, and tell all. I think my clit's getting bigger too. Punishment for renting a stud and getting my dog pregnant. The doctor said your hormone levels are within normal ranges for a woman your age. But a true girlfriend shouldn't have said, If you turn into a man, I'm history. She also said, You don't want me, you want to *be* me. And she said, Lips that touch wangers will never touch mine. She was a girlfriend not a poet.

My dog squats to pee. She has a pointed little vulva. She lets me watch her poop. When I'm on the toilet, she sometimes comes in for a drink, sniffs delicately, then wanders back out.

Just wondering where you were, she always says. She instinctively stays close to me, but I'm not sure it makes her happy like it should.

I always wash before medicating. I undressed and got into the tub. I hate it when I'm trapped in a room with my dirty underwear. She'll sniff it, then drink, either from the bowl or warm water from the bath. Come here, I said, hooking my chin over the edge of the tub.

When she licks my face, I say, Let Mommie be your puppy. Sometimes I imagine her tongue is shaving my upper lip. It's what a girlfriend should've done. I don't know why I wanted her to be my girlfriend. Or any girlfriend. Yes I do. She was going to make me beautiful.

Everything around me is pretty. Especially when I'm on my bed. Gauzy winter light from north-facing curtainless windows, dead tree branches making whispery shadows on white walls, inky blue toner on B&W framed photos of dead trees from another dead year, everything quiet, frozen and dormant. Stiff dried stalks of wheat bleached white, kernels hard and fat, standing upright in a white urn. My shelves are beautiful too, pale unvarnished oak, and my soft gray rug the color of a dove's breast. & my dog & my girlfriend. Long hair, tinted with both blond and chestnut highlights, huge dark sincere eyes. She stares at me so seriously. The applicator already filled. I lifted my leg, exposed it from under the sheet, hadn't shaved for 2 days, she licked carefully around my ankle. When her tongue hit the stiff thorny stubble, she moved down to my foot, between each toe. I sat up on the side of the bed, legs spread, and said go ahead. She didn't even sniff. She went into the kitchen for a drink. Then she came back and said you never want to go on walks anymore, always in bed.

She said I kicked her out of bed in my sleep every night. Then said she wouldn't sleep where a man had squirted. Forgetting I washed the sheets daily. Everything has to be white, bleached and dry. It's an insidious bacteria, craving warmth and moisture. Don't we all. So she caught my infection anyway.

Dirty bitch, she said. I looked at my dog, my dog looked at me.

Two feet on the floor, the rest of her body in bed with me, she was watching me inseminate myself for yeast infection. I used to roll my dog over and say, you have hair where I don't, and no hair where I do. Armpits, groin, all nude. Now? We're almost even. If I'm not a man, maybe I'm a dog. I could've been my girlfriend's dog. I'd be a beautiful dog. In that case, my dog wants to know why *I'm* allowed on the bed and *she's* not. Look, bitch, you want to be *me*? I used her old insemination tube and gave her a shot of yeast medication. I heard you can use yogurt too. She ordinarily loves yogurt. She said, You can't be the father of my puppies.

Everyone's afraid I'll do anything to be related to them.

To make it up to her, I'll let her almost nab a squirrel, but she's not allowed to go all the way. I don't want her catching some disease then giving it to me. As punishment, we're both getting spayed next month after we finish our periods.

Caught

Breathless, still shirtless, familiar taste of blood still in his mouth, 7 a.m., parked beside the chain link fence he usually never even glances at. He always thought his days leaning against a chain fence, waiting to take some swings, were over. But now he moves directly, without a flicker, a bare-chested man on a city sidewalk beside early rush traffic, unsurprised at himself, also not surprised at his lack of surprise. He opens his trunk, heads for his catcher's mitt. Swings around, standing in the gutter, his back to the car, mitt clutched to his chest. Some cars pass, faces turn toward him, then they're gone so quickly. He sits on the curb to replace his shoes with cleats, metal spikes, veterans of real games that counted.

I barely know Mario but followed him into a dark, blank-faced club—how long ago, only eight hours? Was blinded on the inside by colored neon, deafened by stereo thump, suffocated by pressing hot bodies. But was I stunned?

A hardball is jammed in the deepest corner of his trunk, tucked inside a fielder's mitt. He needs them both, digs them out, holds the almost-black fielder's mitt between his knees while he rubs the ball into the catcher's mitt. Heavy, smooth strokes—he grinds the ball into the dark stain in the padded pocket, both a necessity and a ritual before a game.

Mario was immediately sucked into the very center of the heartbeat—the knot of bodies on the dance floor. I never saw him again. The room breathed for me, pulled and pushed my diaphragm and ribs, prodded my heart with a heavy fist. And the lights throbbed. From every corner of the ceiling, from the walls, embedded into the floor: lights. A glob of color hanging from the center of the ceiling, mostly red like new blood, but also blue, teasing glimmers of green. Spurting color. The strands of neon were strings for puppet dancers. A room made out of rhythm.

Gravel crunches underfoot as he turns in his tracks and moves alongside the fence toward the gate. He isn't afraid. Not of this. Neither losing a game nor a hissing crowd nor hard words nor freak injury terrified him on a baseball field. If his heart is straining now, and if he's sweating too heavily and he can't seem to swallow, it is not because he's squeezing under the chain lock, crawling onto the dirty, ill-kept field. No bases, no plate, just hollows in the dirt, but he heads for his place in front of the backstop.

Not possible that I was ever afraid on a ballfield. Even squatting behind the man with the bat, never once thought: he could kill me by mistake. I was 20-years-old and life was slow motion, plenty of time, like catching a pop foul: head back, eyes up, watching the speck of a ball arcing gracefully over, peaking, curving back toward earth, toward me, lifting my legs without effort, matching the flight of the ball with my circling, twirling dance. They said I had instinct. Understood the pattern of the game. Never stopped to think about what it was I was supposed to understand so innately. Kids, just fooling around, my roomie Rick wearing his jockstrap like a gas mask, jumping out of the bushes to scare tourists. And our fast-back contests—like a simple game of catch, but throw it back as fast as possible, catch him before he's ready, try to hit him with the ball, honing our 20-year-old reflexes. Then eel-tag or underwater lobster fights, illicitly using the pool after midnight ("Stay outta the pool, boys, it'll sap your strength"), so we had to glide around without splashing, without breaking the smooth surface of the water. He was a journeyman infielder but my place was always in front of the backstop.

I wouldn't let anything I couldn't see get behind me—I kept the wall at my back. I held a wet beer bottle. I may have sipped from it, but never with my eyes shut. People dancing, lights flashing, ice plinking, conversation pushing under a steady bass and cymbal upbeat. Just people dancing and talking, a kiss here, slapped face there, dark booths with black-outlined human forms, two heads together. That's all. Hard to breathe at my own rate without hiccuping—a hard jerk from my stomach which bounced my head—so I didn't fight the rhythm any more, breathed when everyone else did. We sucked the air out of the room together, blew it back in. The walls moved in and out. I didn't search long for women. Just slender men, like grass blowing with the swirling wind on the dance floor, or sleek seals you'd like to swim with, cutting still water while holding on, feeling the muscles which propel them.

From the bathroom came a queen with a round ass in a mini-skirt, a tight flat sweater, smooth hairless arms and legs which looked yellow in the neon. A thin boy in jeans took the queen's hands out on the dance floor. The music was elastic, pushing forward and holding back. Finally each beat was both a relief and a headache. And the boy smiled, turned his partner around, still holding only the yellow hands. They were still for a moment, a second, a long flexible fraction of time, and the downbeat hit as the round ass in its purple skirt pressed into the front of the boy's tight crotch. Their hips made one rhythm. Heavy, grinding, rolling strokes, jeans and skirt, ass and crotch. I couldn't catch a breath, I must've been dead, for a while at least.

The music changed and someone shrieked, a long full-moon howl. Everyone cheered. The mini-skirt was goosed, turned and slapped the boy with yellow palm and jeweled fingers. He never lost his grin. They grinned together and left, together, holding hands. He opened the door and the skirt stepped outside. My beer bottle, still full, still wet and cold, was pressed to my face. I'm not sure for how long. I never noticed any numbness—of either hand, my cheeks nor forehead. Not like holding that icepack to my mouth, flat on my back, game over, my own syrupy blood draining down my throat, watching my teammates shower, moving like demons in and out of the steam. Their hair darkened and stuck to their skin, making patterns on their legs and asses as the water streamed down. The radio was on, harsh bounce of rock, but they never danced—would slip on the slick shower floor. They talked about the rhythm of the pitcher who'd broken their bats that day, his mesmerizing pump and throw. The steam was made of their sweat and breath, thick and sweet, turning to water on the metal lockers, and on me. I wiped their wetness from my own skin. Their hair dripped and the steam was white and the yellow water gurgled down the drain.

The field is cool, feels ready for rain or just damp air left over from a foggy dawn. His jaw aches. Another guy runs laps, circling this field and another—around the back of one backstop, across first base, into right center, over the line and he touches left center on the far field, tags the worn-out hole marking third base, around the backstop and heads for first again—wearing gray shorts and a pale gold shirt, damp in front, down the middle, not a big guy, footsteps marked by a grunt from his chest, then he takes in air on the upbeat, perfect rhythm.

The catcher waits as the other guy comes across from the opposite diamond, across this outfield, toward this backstop. The runner's hair is damp-dark, he doesn't look up, doesn't break stride, comes around the backstop where the catcher halts him with his arm in his path, catches him with a mitt in his gut, then grabs the runner's arm with his throwing hand. "We're gonna play catch."

"Hey, no, I'm—"

The catcher is pressing the mitt into the guy's chest. He squirms like a bug being pinched between thumb and forefinger.

"Leave me alone." He tries to punch a knee into the catcher's balls.

The catcher shakes him. Can't do much else—he's only actually holding one of the guy's arms, but still mashing the mitt against the guy's chest with his own glove-hand. Shaking upsets the runner's effort, has to lower his knee to stand on two feet. But he swings a fist. So the catcher moves close against him. His arm flails, the catcher saying in his ear, "I bite, kid. Now let's play." The runner stops struggling. "Throwing and catching is all we're going to do. Just throw and catch, throw and catch, keep it going."

The runner puts his hands over the mitt, holds it against his chest by himself. So the catcher removes his hand, both his hands, begins to back away. The runner stares. His mouth is sucked hard against his teeth. He hurries to push his hand into the glove as the catcher shoots the ball toward him, backs him up to second base where he stays when shouted at to stop. That's where he'll take the throw-down from the catcher. He's around twenty years old. He bites the middle finger of the mitt and stares at the catcher over the top.

I didn't dance.

For a long time no one approached, no one asked. The tunes seemed to end faster and faster, and with the beginning of each, the renewed possibility of being asked, being taken, being led, being dragged to the dance floor. I mouthed my neat "no," practiced my placid shrug, watched the partners change, redistribute. They traded mid-dance, everyone danced with everyone else.

He had gray sideburns and matching gray wavy hair combed straight back, a gold chain at his throat, and he appeared at my side, from nowhere, touched my arm with ten fingers, raised his slim gray eyebrows and said, "Dance?"

Did my body relax a moment, seem to be swayed by him? *No!* His fingers tightened, tugging slightly, and he smiled. Perfect teeth, beautiful caps, not unlike my own phony set. Did he get his for the same reason? Did he deserve it? I wrenched my arm away. Turned my back. Dizzy. Out of breath. My jaw ached.

The music became faster, erratic, unpredictable, unsteady, unsatisfied, and the lights did the same for the sake of any deaf dancers, or those going deaf. But I was aware of something steady, calm, clear, cool, confident: Pat's eyes, watching me through the people. I kept glancing back, catching him looking, but his eyes never flitted away. Steady and strong. And I glanced back more often, and looked longer, and leaned against the wall. And when I thought to smile, and the thought was still only a shadow on my lips, he split the crowd to join me. He wore number twenty-one on a baseball sweatshirt.

He was a professional, hard-throwing catcher and the inexperienced 20-year-old across the diamond from him hides behind the

*fielder's mitt. The catcher is throwing hard enough to bruise the
bone.*

My nickname, bone-bruiser, as a promising minor league catcher.
The game was a rhythm in me. Catch and throw or swing and
connect. I was more than good. Tobacco in my cheek, running,
hitting, sliding, and never swallowed the bitter, brown lump.
The beer was good after the game. Sometimes vodka. A bottle
bobbing around in the pool with us, just fooling around, skinny-
dipping after curfew with my roomie Rick, his hair plastered
down, paddling softly after the bottle, quiet liquid darkness, a
closeness only ballplayers can know, underwater friendship,
like the soft sounds of seals playing. When they taught us to
slide head-first, they said slide like a seal down a shoot. But I
had to go home one summer to get a new mouth and new jaw, a
few new teeth and a neat seam across my tongue. They said I
deserved it.

I had been resting my chin on the mouth of my beer bottle,
and as Pat approached I raised my head. I knew what to say:
"Baseball," and the pulsating madness faded with his slow
smile.

"Pardon?"

"You play? I mean, your jersey ...."

"Oh. Just a company softball team. We played tonight."

I could see his skin beneath the red, blue and orange tints
flashing on his cheeks. No make-up. No jewelry. No lilt in his
walk. I saw the number twenty-one and short hair and ears and
simple face and bright mouth and soft eyes, and I cried a little—
at least my eyes were wet, obviously with relief.

"I played professional."

"You mean real live hardball? The big money?"

"Well, I played in the minors." Momentarily I was sickened
slightly by the mixture of my honesty with the severe lights and

confusing music, as though the heat and noise and smoke hovering under the heart-beat strobe were laughing, as though I'd made a long-awaited confession.

"I probably would've made it to the big leagues. I can't actually remember giving up on it. But ...."

He looked away, scanning the dance floor. "You don't have to explain. Most of us understand."

"You do?"

He turned back toward me. "My name's Pat."

"Gary." We shook hands, more than one shake, then he tapped his brow with a yellow scarf he took from his pocket. "Let's get outta here, okay? Kinda hot tonight. Kinda tight in here."

There was sweat on my neck. I agreed with him. It was too hot in there.

His yellow-shirted partner taking the throw-down at second base is ducking, but hasn't run away. The catcher nearly falls down while throwing. The ball flies at the other guy like a big rock thrown anonymously out of an angry mob. Catching it nearly sits him down backwards. But he returns it. Doesn't stall, doesn't lob it high in the air or roll angry grounders. The other guy throws without emotion. Only when he catches, seconds before it reaches his head, do his white teeth show, tight between his lips, set together on edge, and his eyes shut and his head goes down behind the mitt. The ball slams home, pushes the glove back into his face. The catcher is throwing zingers. Still rising as they reach second base. And even as the twenty-year-old wiggles out of his drenched yellow shirt, the catcher can't wait, won't slow down, has to keep the rhythm, can't fight momentum. The other guy has his mitt in his teeth, pulling the yellow shirt over his head, and it's stuck there, inside-out on his head with the glove still in his mouth, but the catcher throws anyway. The guy turns his back and catches the ball between his shoulder blades.

It doesn't sound like a hand slapping flesh, but it does slap, bites and leaves a red birthmark on his skin. The catcher is sorry for that. But the other guy finishes removing his shirt, turns and faces home plate with his twenty-year-old chest, hairless and shiny wet, heaving in and out. Hopefully anger and not fatigue. The catcher tenses in preparation. The twenty-year-old picks up the ball.

We found a basement under a hospital, down the block from the club, filled with steam from the hospital laundry, but empty, three a.m. I'd walked the night air for over an hour, breathing gallons, cool and damp, and heard Pat's soft footsteps beside me as we talked in late-night voices. The things people talk about: great teams, memorable players, bad trades. I felt him listening carefully. More carefully than he should've, or maybe my imagination. When he spoke, I tried to be interested, but was distracted by the thud of my heart, my deep slow breathing, and his beside me, our footsteps setting the same pace.

Then he said, "See there," pointing to the basement window at ground level, a yellow glow. "Let's go inside."

"Someone's there."

"Not at this hour. They leave the light on. The machines are running."

"How do you know?"

He smiled and took me to the window, easy to open, and he touched my elbow lightly as I put my legs through. It was a drop into the basement, and he followed, wanting me to take his legs and catch him as he came through the window. But I said, "No, jump like I did," and I turned to see where we were.

The machines droned. I already felt slimy from the steam, once again found it hard to breathe. Once again too noisy for common talk. Through cloudy yellow windows in the dryers, I could see hospital sheets tumble. Pat took a pole and shut the window.

"I felt better outside walking."

But, again, Pat only smiled.

I said, "I left with you because ...." I stopped.

I mumbled, "I never said I ...."

I whispered, "I don't know."

Pat found a radio. He didn't have to search long. Just walked right over to it and clicked it on.

"No. I'm sick of music."

"I'll put it on low."

"We left there because the music was too loud."

Pat smiled, but not at me. Smiled gently at his hand on the radio dial. He said, "Did we? I forgot." He didn't turn it off. I heard it through the tiny speaker as though the club up the street piped their music here.

"The music gave me a headache."

"This'll be okay."

We waited, the steam and most of the basement between us, until Pat picked a song. Slow but bouncy. He moved his hips. I watched without moving—uninterested or uninvolved or unamazed or disappointed or undecided or dead.

He put his arms over his head, flowing like underwater grass. I didn't move and he came no closer. Our shirts were wet. I saw his, felt mine. He took his off and resumed the dance. I also removed my shirt. He was very thin. There was only one light— the yellow light bulb at the ceiling which we'd seen from the street. It cast shadows under his collar bones, between his ribs. His flat tummy had little hair, but there was some, dark and wet around his navel.

He came no closer throughout the whole dance. He danced alone. The song ended and an advertisement began. Pat turned to change the station or to turn it off. Then changed his mind and left it. He picked up his shirt and came through the steam toward me. Up close, I saw that his skin was slick. So was mine. But neither of us wiped ourselves.

Pat said, "I really don't like that place either."

"Why did you go?"

"Why did you?"

"Someone from work took me. I mean, I followed him ... in my car. He said I may find it's what I'm looking for, or it may not be after all." I laughed, a strange sound there. "Maybe I already found out, though, a long time ago."

Pat didn't laugh, but he smiled. The smell in the laundry room was like something rotting there. He said, "Gary, let's be honest with each other."

Wish I could say I was surprised, even shocked. "Haven't we been?"

"I love baseball. I'm a real fan."

"Oh yeah?" I said dully.

"Isn't there something mythical or mystic about the game? The legends, the half-truths, the hero worship, the sanctity of the clubhouse, and all that? A whole world you can escape into." The steam seemed to shift. The machines stopped, the sheets made one final flop. Somewhere a fan still swished, though barely a whisper, and the radio was playing music again, thick with boogaloo percussion. Pat said, "I've always wanted to meet a real player."

Caught.

"It's been a long time."

A long time since I was on third base, a triple lashed into left center, then got trapped off the bag with Ricky, bleary-eyed, at the plate: In his sick weakness—only twelve hours after something had happened underwater that I'd thought neither of us could exactly remember—the booze was suddenly to blame. But, if true, he wouldn't've had to smash my face with the bat. Yet, just minutes before they dragged me away, there I was on third base. I loved being twenty-years-old on third base. The last time I was on third. The last time I loved being twenty-years-old.

The catcher has extended to his full motion: crouch for the catch, rise and throw, using arm, legs and body. The ball is like a rope between him and the man on second, twenty years old. The catcher's jaw aches. Probably his teeth are clenched.

The steam began to clear but never left all together. The window dripped. Dawn was gray. Pat danced, then stopped. Resting, breathing heavily. When he bent at the waist, profile to me, I could see how narrow he was just above the belt. He put his hands on his knees and his ribcage expanded and contracted.

I yawned and he laughed. Then he checked his watch. "The morning shift will be here soon, at six-thirty."

"We'd better go."

"We'd better hurry." He turned the radio up. The tiny speaker distorted the music into a mash of electric sounds, nothing soft or bouncy to it. Hard and coarse like sand in my mouth.

Pat came toward me again. We stood facing. "How about a game, slugger." He unbuckled his pants, let them drop, wiggled his hips to remove the underwear. His clothes shackled his legs from the knees down. I flexed my jaw without parting my lips. I thought I felt the pin there, for the first time. They told me I'd never feel it.

He was like silk yet the music was nails. I crouched like a catcher, squatted on the floor, held my balance with my fingertips pressing against the cement in front of my feet. At first he shuddered, quivered, then the jolts became a rhythm. Pump, throw, catch, return, and again. Like waves, smooth rollers, in and out. The water swelled but never broke, never crashed white and foamy. I was out beyond the breakers, swimming with a seal, born to slip and slide, glide and dive, run races, play tag, throw and catch, touch each bag with the right toe, never stumbling off stride, never fooled by the pick-off. Trapped off base. Caught. My roomie, Rick, sluggish and mesmerized, still in the box, still at the plate, hypnotized by the rhythm of the rundown, pitcher to third to catcher to short. But *my* reflexes weren't dulled, put my head down and broke for home, past the surprised catcher—out of position too far up the line. I was home free, sliding face first, only my own man waiting at the plate to greet me, to embrace me ... but he cocks his bat and takes a full swing—

On hands and knees, I bit down. Hard. The scream wasn't mine this time. The scream that ends it. I spit blood and shut my eyes and grabbed my hair, and spit again. We doubled, head-to-head on the floor where he vomited, yellow acid. I spit blood.

Then I left through the window, left him crying on the floor, his cheek lying flat in the yellow slime and saliva-blood, crying.

Everyone had said I deserved it.

Each throw pounds dust from the pocket of the catcher's mitt. He chokes on it, his eyes water, but they don't stop. The catcher keeps digging the ball out of his mitt and the other keeps sending it back. When he blinks, there's grit and dirt in his tears. The other guy is still throwing hard, harder than he did at first, as hard as a twenty-year-old body can. Throws with the strength in his legs and the long muscle down his back. The catcher grunts as he receives it, catches each one near his head, around his eyes, in front of his mouth. He tries to throw back before the other guy can recover from his follow-through. But the other guy is quick— getting quicker—and the catcher's motion is getting awkward. He's throwing harder than is possible for someone who's busy protecting his head, his face, his nose and mouth. Dig and throw and recover and return. They're both yelling, grunting shouts with each throw—not words, the voices of their bodies. Wind-up, release, get set to catch. Someone has to finish it, let the end happen. The boy throws and the catcher shuts his eyes but still sees everything. As though the ball is standing still and he's the one hurling his head toward it, to catch the moment of splintering bones and spurting blood, and teeth that rattle loose. His head snaps back.

Adrenalin

1.

It wasn't fear, frigidity or reclusiveness that made Maureen wait so long to have her first lover, who turned out to be Grant. Then she didn't have time to be melancholy about the years without love because the relationship with Grant progressed too quickly and intensely. She didn't even pause to fret about inexperience. Giddy instinct took over, for a while. Her virginity was fairly apparent for a few days, but she put it aside, ignoring or not even noticing the initial clumsiness. At least half of the time sex was her idea, and it became easier for her, although never climactic. She wasn't worried about that. She was too astonished by the obvious effect she had on *him*: the sweat on his forehead and temples, his deep panting and drowsy expression, his eyes half closed but still staring at her, his mouth involuntarily puckered because he had hyperventilated.

"I want a picture of this—the way your face looks right now," she said once, her own face not even an inch away because he was lying on top of her, resting afterwards.

"Let's just hope you'll see me this way often enough," he said, still a little out of breath. "You won't *need* a picture."

"But if I had one I could look at it when we're *not* in bed."

"Why?"

She didn't have an answer that time, so she just wrapped her legs around his back.

She worked part-time in a hospital, billing, and he was a

musician in a band that played several nights a week. But except for his gigs and her job, they were always together, either at his studio or her apartment. She wrote letters to him while she was at work, then brought them home to him and watched him read, waiting for him to look up at her, the few seconds before he pulled her close and kissed her.

When she was younger and lived at home with her parents, her mother used to spend the whole summer canning fruits and making jelly. The kitchen would be thickly filled with the pungent combination of hot fruit and too much sugar. Smelling it, even just walking through the kitchen and quickly out the back door, made her stomach burn and legs feel weak. That first summer with Grant she finally felt it again, even though his faint smell and taste was musky or salty. It happened when he looked at her a certain way.

His face was almond-shaped, thin, without prominent cheekbones, but his eyes, mouth and teeth were large, his lips full. His hair was straw texture and shaggy and hid his ears which stuck out slightly from the sides of his head. His chin was narrow and his neck long. She often watched his mouth when he talked. He had several different smiles. A few times she tried to describe one she liked, to get him to do it again, but although he tried to follow her description, it never came out quite right.

"I want a picture of you," she said again one day. She was dressing for work and he was half asleep in bed, having gotten in at 2 the night before. "Not like this," he mumbled.

"No," she laughed. "I mean just you, smiling or whatever. I need a picture on my dresser and one in my wallet so I can look at you while I'm at work or when you're at a gig."

"You sure it won't excite you too much? His groggy voice was muffled in the pillow, but his eye crinkled and laughed.

"If I'm lucky!" she giggled.

She bought some oak picture frames at a thrift shop, cleaned the glass parts and stained the wood. But the frames were laid aside for a few weeks when Grant suggested they get married and have just one place to live. They did it as soon as they could get blood tests and a license. Maureen quit her job, which she hated, and bought a camera.

"I never needed a camera before, but now I do."

"Why?"

"Now I'm with you and I don't want to *miss* any of it."

At first she just shot photos of him while he was busy practicing his string bass or reading the newspaper or playing a game of scrabble or chess with her. Then she began to pose him, and she again tried to describe the expressions she wanted.

Once Grant remarked that it made him a little uncomfortable to have pictures of himself all over, like seeing his own head stuffed and mounted over the fireplace.

"I know, I used to wonder why hunters do that," she said. "But now I understand. Imagine being out hunting, and for days you don't see anything but footprints and turds. Deer are so beautiful and elusive that when a hunter finally gets one, he wants to preserve that extraordinary instant when he first saw it staring at him from a thicket—startled, alert, flooded with adrenalin."

He laughed and said, "Just don't start taking the camera to bed."

"Very funny."

But they didn't go to bed as often.

There were always pictures of him still on the film in the camera, and a finished roll of film at the drug store being developed into snapshots, and last week's snapshots spread out on a table—with a magnifying glass handy—constantly arranged and rearranged in order of best-to-worst, while negatives of the best ones from a previous batch were already at the photo shop being enlarged to 8x10 or 11x14. In the meantime there were finished enlargements waiting for frames and frames waiting for varnish or paint to dry. Then there were the already framed photographs leaning against the back of the couch as she analyzed the walls to find the best way to add the newly framed photos to those already hung. She started using the savings she'd had before they were married to buy more lenses and instruction books. And she suggested they go places to use different settings. She threw together a picnic lunch and they went to a lake but she hardly ate anything. She took pictures of Grant feeding the ducks, sharing his sandwich unintentionally with a goose, slipping on the mud and duck shit near the water, laughing at his own wet behind. But Maureen didn't laugh. She had to concentrate on holding the camera still.

Then she moped when he wouldn't sit for portraits anymore. "Honey, c'mon," he said. "Don't you have enough pictures yet?"

"None of these seem good enough."

"Gee, sorry, maybe you need a new model."

"No, Grant, it's not your fault! It must be mine. I don't seem to be getting the exact right moment, these pictures just don't *do* anything for me. I'm losing things!"

"You're not losing anything. I'm still here."

"You still don't understand, do you."

In the second year Grant's group, a dance band called *The King's Gentlemen*, got an agent and started booking steady jobs for higher pay. Grant and Maureen moved to a larger house with one extra bedroom. "This is your photography room, okay, honey?"

He suggested she could go find some tables or a desk at thrift shops, and she said she probably would, but many of the cartons of photographs and albums were never unpacked. She did hang most of the framed pictures, and spent several weeks rearranging them. The band was rehearsing more, so Grant was out afternoons and nights. When he was home they still played games and sometimes made love, and he often saw her lenses on the kitchen table lying on soft cloth with a bottle of cleaning solution nearby. Then one night he came home from playing at a nightclub and found her packing the lenses in styrofoam bits and sealing the boxes.

It was Maureen's idea for them to buy their first television, and while they were shopping he decided to get a VCR also. Maureen taped a few shows while Grant was at work, and they watched them together after midnight. He liked to make pop-corn when he got home, and they became involved in a few serial-dramas, but during the summer only the reruns were on so she stopped taping shows, then they never went back to watching when the fall season began. The band was heavily booked and even had a tour coming up in the spring. Grant realized Maureen hadn't done much of anything for over a year. He couldn't imagine how she filled her days.

2.

When Grant came home from tour, she apologized for the mess, but he just said, "I'm the kind of guy who may be standing up to his ears in horseshit, but just thinks: there must be a pretty little pony around here somewhere. It was something he'd said before.

He came in and leaned his bass in the corner as Maureen turned the television off, then he hugged her. She stayed for a moment, but squirmed and said, "I'm being choked." When he released her, she started picking up newspapers and dirty dishes, throwing pillows back onto the couch, straightening slip-covers.

He cleared his throat. "Well ... you had some time to be alone and think. Feeling any better?"

She touched a pimple on her forehead. "I'm twenty-nine and still breaking out."

He smiled.

"Everything's the same," she said. She looked around. "Just messier."

"I like it—it's home. He tried to continue smiling. "So what'd you do all week?"

"I already told you—nothing, not a damn thing. You have a right to be mad. I'm a lazy slob, I guess."

"No, honey—maybe you just needed a rest. He went into the bedroom and threw his jacket on the bed. The bed wasn't made, but it seldom was. He usually slept until at least noon and she'd gotten into the habit of going to bed early at night. Why make the bed just a few hours before it'll be torn apart again?

She was still standing in the living room, hugging one of the sofa pillows against her belly. He went to her to hold her, and bent to kiss her, but she started talking against his mouth. He said, "What?"

She sat suddenly on the couch, still holding the pillow. "I'm sorry about your cashew nuts. I ate them all."

"They weren't just mine. I'm glad you enjoyed them."

"You bought them—"

He noticed an empty packing carton on the floor and the photo albums stacked on the coffee table. The top album was open, but a section of newspaper had been dropped over the page of photos. Also on the table were two magnifying glasses of different sizes propped upright in an empty juice glass. He picked up a paperback book that was halfway under the sofa. It was a pulp romance, printed on recycled newsprint. She reached for it so he handed it to her while he said, "Really, I'm glad you ate them—I was getting tired of them and wanted to finish them so we could get something else. Look, I've got a check here— what treat shall we get for ourselves?"

"I'll get fat and you'll hate me."

He laughed and sat beside her, pulling her close. He kissed her cheek and her neck. "Impossible," he murmured.

"Which—that I'll get fat or you'll hate me."

"Both. He kissed her ear and she shivered. He laughed again. "Tickle?"

She sighed and leaned against him for a moment, then sprang up to remove a dirty coffee cup from the window sill. "How'd you get home—I thought you were going to call from the depot."

"I called from Riverside last night but couldn't get you, so Dave dropped me off."

Maureen parted the curtain to look out the window. "I was going to wash the car and didn't," she said. "That's another thing I didn't do. I'm terrible."

"No you're not." He leaned back, stretched both arms along

the back of the sofa and crossed his legs. "It's okay anyway because you do a lousy job on the car."

"That's a nice thing to say." She glared at him.

"I was kidding, honey—come on!" he laughed, then sighed and closed his eyes. "Come here, Maureen."

"Just a second. She went into the bedroom and came back holding some envelopes. "I opened your mail. I'm sorry. Are you mad?"

Grant stood, went to her, took the envelopes and tossed them aside. "I missed you," he said, "how can I be mad at you. She had her face down against his chest, so he kissed the top of her head. "Especially for such silly things. There's nothing private in my mail—was there anything interesting?"

"A letter from your sister."

"Good. Did you enjoy it?"

She looked up, hitting his chin with her head, then she backed away. "Don't patronize me, Grant. After all, *you* went off and had a great time on tour and I had to stay home alone waiting faithfully while you're out doing God-knows-what."

He didn't say anything for a moment, then took her hand. "Yes, I had a pretty good time on tour, but right now I want to have a *better* time."

They walked together into the bedroom and kissed for a while on the bed, then she turned her head so he kissed her neck while he unbuttoned her shirt. "I'm cold, Grant," she said. She pulled the sheet over herself. He undressed and got in bed beside her. She still had her pants on. "It's good to be home," he said, his mouth on her shoulder. "I missed you and thought about you all the time. She was looking at the ceiling. A thin cobweb floated from the light fixture. "It's all right, Mo, I understand. I'll help with the housework and stuff—you need to do whatever will make you happy again."

"Ha!" She rolled to her belly. He sat beside her and began massaging her back.

"Relax, honey." They were both trembling. "What's the matter?"

"Nothing."

"Do you want me to quit the band and get a job with regular hours?"

"No." He could hardly hear her.

"What can I do for you, Mo, you're all I think about—"

"Stop it!" she shouted. She sat up, kneeling, but kept her back to him. "All right, I'll *tell* you—I thought you wouldn't want to know—okay, I met someone, but nothing *happened*."

He closed his eyes. He felt foolish sitting there naked, and he started to get dizzy. When he opened his eyes he saw her slowly lean forward, lay her forehead on her knees and sob. He stared at her for a long time.

3.

She left four days later. She didn't even take a suitcase, but she put a bar of soap and her toothbrush in her purse. And she took the first apartment she found, which wasn't far away since she'd left on foot, but Grant wouldn't know that. It was a studio down on Adams Avenue. One of the walls was right on the sidewalk—people could look into her window as they walked by, if they wanted to. There was no heat nor electricity yet, no furniture and no phone installed.

She sat on the floor and held her head and thought about the jumbo bottle of aspirin on the bathroom shelf at home. Grant had taken it down every morning, the past three mornings, swallowed a few tablets, washed his face, and come back to the bedroom smiling. He wanted her to get up, get her camera and go to the zoo; get up, grab a coat and her camera and go sailing; get up, find her boots and her camera and go for a hike in the mountains. He had a week vacation before the band started a long booking at a local club. But Maureen wanted to stay in bed. She wanted Grant to sit beside her, instead of pacing back and forth at the foot of the bed, pinching her toes, laughing, fully dressed, sunglasses in his pocket, keys in his hand, saying, "C'mon, where do you want to go for breakfast?"

"Let's just talk, Grant."

"We can do that at the zoo or the beach, anywhere we go."

"I want to talk *here*. Grant, we *have* to talk about it."

He'd only stopped smiling for a second. "There's nothing to talk about."

"How can you say that!"

He was grinning again. "Come on, what do you want to do that's fun for you? That's what you need."

She didn't know how to tell him—what she needed was an adrenalin rush, a sudden one, like her guts were exploding. Every time she thought about what had happened while Grant was on tour, she felt it again, a reminder, a taste. "I want to explain it to you, Grant," she begged.

At first leaving Grant was out of the question—it never entered her mind. The first night he was home from tour, he held her all night like a stuffed bear, and sighed just before going to sleep, but continued to hold her after he slept, just as tightly, while she lay there and thought about what had happened with Paul in the park, or what had *almost* happened—or what had seemed to be something happening while it happened, but if she told anyone, it would immediately become *nothing* as she told it, because, after all, what *had* happened? If anyone filmed it and showed it to an audience, they would all say, "nothing happened." That's what people thought nothing was, and she would've *agreed*, a week ago, but now—how could it be *nothing* when all she could do was think about it?

4.

When Grant was away on tour, Maureen had tried to be more energetic—at least she got up early, read, took deep afternoon naps and stayed up late playing solitaire and watching television. But she had thought a lot about Grant and how she was going to really try to make him happier, first of all by not being in such a funk all the time. Wednesday she decided maybe she should go out and *do* something, like take a bus to the park, but she didn't actually do it until Thursday afternoon. She hadn't taken her camera and didn't miss it as she wandered among fountains and museums and jugglers and goldfish pools, botanical gardens, lawn bowling, rose gardens planted in miniature mazes (which were too simple to become lost in), replica rain forests and deserts, and tourists. It was noisy, but not like crowd sounds at the racetrack or a ballpark. She could hear individual words and individual laughter. It was warm, early spring, and she sat on a bench letting the sun melt her limbs into rubber. She was only half interested in the mime act in a small quad in front of her, but a crowd of tourists had gathered, and Paul was in that crowd. She didn't notice him until he had already come out of the gathering and sat beside her on the bench. Even then she hardly glanced at him. Not until he asked her how she could be at the park on such a beautiful day, watching such a good show, and seem so unhappy.

Then when she turned and looked at him, his eyes were surprisingly close, and that first silent meeting was nearly violent. After that, he talked for a few minutes, unplanned, rambling, but fluent words: His first and last name ... he wondered why she was sad ... she must be a local because she didn't look like a person on a holiday ... being 300 miles from home and on his last day of vacation made him feel uninhibited about coming to meet her and hear her story ... maybe he could cheer her up ... she probably didn't know how pretty she was all alone on this bench as though it was raining and the park empty.

But she hardly heard anything, just sat staring at him. Her left hand was a rigid fist held tight against her body, burying her wedding ring against her stomach. When he asked if she wasn't feeling well, she abruptly said, "No, I'm not well," and it was the truth—her stomach burned. He took her fist away from her body and loosened her fingers so her hand lay flat in his, but she immediately lifted her hand closer to his eyes and pointed to the ring. She didn't stop there. She told him how Grant didn't care what kind of wife she was, never complained if he got a cheese sandwich for dinner five nights in a row because she didn't feel like cooking or cleaning up; and he usually did the dishes so she didn't mind when he broke a glass about once a week; and they played games and even had designed one together once but never bothered to try to sell it; and she'd taught him chess and he taught her backgammon but he'd gotten better than her at chess while she still had to count the lines in backgammon; and sometimes she was a poor sport, sulked and wouldn't finish a game when it was obvious she would lose, so it almost seemed he was happier when she won— he didn't bump her single gammon pieces and warned her about her undefended chessmen. A few times Paul said, "You don't have to tell me this—I understand," but she couldn't stop because none of it sounded like much of an excuse to be unhappy. She even tried to boast about the band and took out a photo from her wallet, but Paul wouldn't look at it.

They walked together all over the park trying to figure out what was happening to them, periodically interrupted by moments of frantic silence, staring at each other, and how many times did one of them say, "What are we going to do?" Then they kept walking, and he gripped her arm as though she might run away. They walked and talked, then groaned aloud in the silences, and laughed because they groaned, but groaned again, and stared at each other in the lengthening shadows. They were in an undeveloped part of the park, beside a construction site where a new theater was being built, surrounded by a temporary fence with metal signs fastened to the chain links: KEEP OUT, CONSTRUCTION AREA, DANGER! Paul kept handing her his business cards. He said she might lose it if he just gave her *one*. She had a stack of them in her pocket, in her fist. He grabbed her shoulders clumsily and pulled her to him. She tried to avoid it, but only turned her head slightly, and he kissed the corner of her mouth, gently, but she remembered it as hysterical, stormy, brutal, because afterwards, when they looked at each other, they were actually afraid. Simultaneously they turned and walked away in opposite directions. Maureen took just a few steps then turned around. It was almost dark. Paul stopped at the corner of the fence just long enough to make a fist and hit the metal sign—Maureen's knees almost buckled, the whole fence rattled, sending the vibration all the way down to where she was still standing, shivering, her own fist in her pocket holding the business cards.

5.

Grant had to move the photo albums so he could put his coffee and cereal bowl on the table in the living room. It was the morning after he'd come home from tour. She watched him open one of the albums, glance at the page, take a sip of coffee and turn two more pages, looking at each quickly. Then she suddenly picked up the whole armload of albums and started to take them back to the extra room. Grant said, "You were really getting good at your photography. How would you like to do some publicity photos for the band—we'll pay you. And it'll give you something to do."

Later he said, "How about if we save all the money from the weddings I've been playing and buy you some darkroom equipment so you could freelance."

And during a silent meal at a restaurant, he said suddenly, "I thought you used to want to be a photographer." She stared at her plate. She didn't need a photograph to remember the cold spring twilight at the park, the distant sounds of traffic and laughter, the force of the kiss which she'd almost avoided—or almost *missed*—and his urgent eyes. She tried to imagine herself lifting a camera and looking through it: at Paul during the moments they'd faced each other in crazed silence. She certainly would've had a picture of him to keep: a picture of his face put off, insulted, turning away—a picture of something else entirely rather than her animated memory of what it *was*.

She looked up at Grant across the linguini with clam sauce that she hadn't touched, and he smiled—the same daring, toothy smile he'd given her the day they'd first met at the racetrack and shared hunches, before she'd ever taken a photograph of it, when she was never listless. If they weren't heatedly discussing horses and jockeys, they'd talked about themselves, as though they had to say everything that day or it would never be said. Then they'd come home together, hot, out of money, and lay on the floor of her apartment without turning on the lights, exploring each other happily. The first knot of adrenalin in her stomach had been so bright, she'd almost vomited ... and now there was no adrenalin at all in the dimly lit restaurant with expensive food on the table. "This is fun," Grant said, and she ran sobbing to the restroom.

Later they took a walk in a tourist development of shops and clubs, and Grant showed her where the band had its next engagement. She took his hand and listened again to him talk about his plans for the band and the records they would make someday, and all the titles for the albums they'd already decided on. She wondered if any of the titles would change if she left him—that's when she first thought about it—and what kind of songs he would write.

At home that night he took her in his arms and kissed her face and neck, opened her blouse and kissed her breasts, slid his hands up her back, his fingertips callused from his bass strings, yet still gentle. But she was tired and weak—she felt as though she'd been crying for a long time, red-eyes and sore stomach—and she lay limp in his arms after he'd undressed her, watching him admire her with his dark eyes, his full mouth, his hands.

It was useless anyway. He turned away from her and lay still, then whispered, "I'm sorry."

"No, I am," she said, whispering too. And they hadn't said anything more.

6.

She dozed a little on the floor of her new apartment, then woke stiff and sweaty. But she didn't go back to the house until after she went to the corner liquor store and bought some cola, a bottle of rum, and a package of paper cups. It was the only drink she knew the ingredients for.

Standing across the street from the house, she checked to make sure Grant was still out getting a haircut and having the car tuned-up, which was where he'd said he was going when he woke her that morning, an hour before she'd actually gotten up and left to find an apartment. She ran across the street, into the alley, and went in the back door, changed her clothes and wrote a note for Grant on the back of an empty envelope: *I'll contact you when I know what I'm going to do*. She thought a while, then added, *Don't worry*.

On the fourth drink, the cola was getting low, so she just used more rum. She wished she'd stuffed some extra pairs of underwear into her purse. How could leaving be so complicated. She hoped she wouldn't have to keep going back and getting things. She could wash out her clothes in the sink, but where could she hide while they were drying—people on the sidewalk might look through her curtainless windows and see her naked in a bare room, a woman obviously waiting for a clandestine meeting with her lover; even though she'd told Paul, "I won't leave my husband"—the last word had seemed plump and middle-aged, and the sentence incredible because she'd never even imagined leaving Grant, and even more incredible now because she *had*. She'd left Grant and Paul didn't even know it—he was 300 miles away and she was alone in a bare room. That meant she *hadn't* left Grant for another man.

That's when she first started picturing them side-by-side, trying to put them in the same room or sit them on the same couch or at the same side of a table across from her. But she couldn't do it. She finished the drink quickly and crumpled the cup, now lying on the floor staring at the ceiling, as though pictures could hang there and look down without falling on her.

It was still easy to see Paul's squinting pale green eyes, his tourist's sunburned nose, the scattered freckles, laugh lines visible even when he wasn't smiling, chapped lips, slightly messy, curly hair. She could even smell his sunscreen and his cottony new shirt and feel the dampness of his palms. And especially she could still hear the desperate or hysterical silences that just remembering made her have to pull her knees to her chest and roll to her side, a delirious agony. She vomited the rum-and-cola, panting—she couldn't wait for it to end, couldn't wait until it started again. Wasn't it, after all, the adrenal gland that loved, and not the heart?

When she pictured Grant, it was the photographs. A few times when they used to have guests, someone would say, "What a great picture of Grant."

"But do you think it *really* looks like him?" she remembered answering—*begging*. She'd thought more about those photographs in the past week than in the past year. Through untrained technique and fear of losing details in a blur, she had made him hold up a finger or pencil or his bow so she could focus on a vertical line. Clarity was all she asked of her photography, because how could memory ever be as exact or permanent? And she'd assumed each of the photographs *was* Grant, smiling or serious, amused or pensive—weren't they all the Grants she'd thought she'd ever known? But obviously, she now knew, not the first one. Where was *that* Grant, the one who'd looked at *her*, not at a camera—what was *he* doing now? Perhaps looking at a photograph of her (if he even had one, she didn't know). Suddenly she couldn't remember what he looked like, looking at her, or was it really all that sudden? The elusive Grant—that deer alive in the thicket before being stuffed and mounted, before the bottomless liquid eyes were turned into polished glass. It *wasn't* the same animal up on the wall. Isn't that why hunters continued to go back into the woods with their rifles re-loaded?

7.
Paul sounded delighted when she called collect from the drug store. "Maureen? I just can't believe it's you."

"Well, it is."

"I know—and it's great. I want to see you."

"When can you get here?"

"As soon as possible—Saturday."

"Not soon enough," she said.

He chuckled. "You know, I kept trying to explain to myself what happened to us."

"I know. Me too. It's hard."

"I know. We have to see each other again."

"The sooner the better." Maureen took a deep breath. "Tomorrow. Can you arrange it?"

"Of course, honey, don't worry."

"Don't call me that."

"Honey? Why?"

"Just don't ... please. Tomorrow? What time should I meet you?"

"God, Maureen, I'm glad you called. I kept wondering if you would ever call or if you lost all the cards or threw them away."

"I didn't. Call me back when you get a time and flight number. As soon as you can—I'm at a pay phone."

"You sound sort of upset, what's wrong?"

"Nothing—everything'll be okay when you get here."

"That's right. This is great. Okay, okay, I'll call right back, don't go anywhere—God, I don't want to hang up, I'm afraid I'll lose you!"

"Oh Paul," she groaned.

Once again she stood across the street to see if Grant was home. It was hours later, almost dusk, so he couldn't still be having the same haircut, but the car wasn't in the driveway. She hurried as she unpacked all her lenses and loaded them into her camera bag, but again she didn't take any extra underwear.

She waited at the airport in the back row of plastic seats. Her camera bag was beside her feet, the camera inside loaded. It was Friday, so the airport was crowded, but not noisy. The other people sitting in the plastic chairs rustled newspapers or talked softly to each other. When the announcement of Paul's arrival came, she got up quickly and walked to the rear of the area, in the far right-hand corner, before any of the passengers came through the doors. She had found a place between a trash receptacle and a plastic potted tree. Several people stared at her as she took her camera out and replaced the regular lens with a more powerful one. Then she focused on the door and watched the passengers file past in her viewfinder. She picked up Paul and stayed with him. He was carrying a small overnight bag and had a light jacket over his arm. He was smiling the whole time, his chin lifted and eyes alert as he searched the waiting room for her. His smile never faded, but the jousting crowd kept momentarily blocking her view as his head bobbed among other people who were already finding each other, hugging or shaking hands or kissing while they still clutched their bags. He looked young and clean and excited and stood on one of the plastic chairs, still smiling—he had dimples and his eyes crinkled—searching for her, thinking of her, wanting her. He panned the room slowly and as his face came around toward her, she closed her eyes, squeezed the camera and felt the deep satisfying click. She left while he was still eagerly, excitedly looking for her.

She didn't bother stopping at the apartment to pick up what was left of the rum or the package of paper cups. The business cards were there still too—she'd taken them out and left them in a strewn pile while she was rechecking her lenses the night before.

Grant's car was parked in the driveway, slightly askew, and the lights were on inside the house. She watched him through a window for a while. He was reading, sitting in the big reclining chair, but for a long time he didn't turn a page. Finally he turned back a few pages and read a paragraph over, tracing the lines with his index finger, nodded and flipped forward again. She stepped softly onto the porch, opened the door and slipped inside. Grant snapped the recliner upright and came flying toward her, but stopped short a few feet away. "Mo! Are you all right?"

"I've been missing something," she said, "and I want it back."

She dropped the camera bag and looked around. The couch and coffee table were piled with newspapers, dirty dishes on top of that. Clothes, both his and hers, were slung over the backs of chairs. The house plants were dry and drooping, a few dead leaves had fallen on the tabletops. And there were shoes everywhere, all over the floor, some with socks stuffed inside. Grant was barefoot.

"God, look at all this shit!" She kicked a shoe under the sofa. She lifted her camera bag, unzipped it and emptied the contents on the floor between their feet. Grant had to jump backwards as a heavy lens hit his toes. Then he bent and picked it up. The domed blue eye of the lens had been smashed in. He picked up the other lenses, one by one. They were all shattered, and the camera itself had been bashed open. As Maureen looked down at the equipment, a few tears fell directly from her eyes to the junk without running down her cheeks. But when she looked up again, at him, at least she could see better. He was holding a lens, smiling at her—another of his smiles she'd never gotten on film and thought she'd lost forever.

The Dog Doesn't Care and the Woman's Too Sleepy

He was sleeping poorly anyway. At first he thought someone had thrown a party and the noise outside was two drunks walking home. It would've been a block party and he hadn't been invited. His wife would've said, Can you blame them? She was sleeping soundly, as usual.

In a matter of seconds he knew they weren't drunk. His wife woke but didn't move, her voice drowsy, "What's going on?"

"Someone's getting killed," Charlie said, kneeling upright in bed. He crawled to the open window near the foot of the bed. He'd left his glasses in the bathroom.

Two people were coming down the long driveway from the apartments across the street. They were just blurs to Charlie. "Help me see," he said to Sheila. She stretched and rolled over, parted the curtain and looked out the window beside her pillow.

One of the two people was crying. The other was shouting.

"He's killing her," Charlie said.

"No he's not." Sheila yawned. "And it's a man."

"Which one!"

"Both." She was still on her belly, her chin propped on the window sill. The dog moved around in its bed but didn't get up and didn't bark.

"I never heard anyone sound like that," Charlie said. "I've never heard that kind of cry. You're right. He's not crying for pain."

The crying was so loud it was hard to hear the other man.

"There—did you get that!" Charlie said.

"What?" Sheila had dozed off.

"He told him, you're a sick sick sick man, and the crying one said, I know, I know."

"I can't hear anything," Sheila said. Her window wasn't open.

Charlie ran his fingers through his hair. It stood on end. He still had a lot of hair. He wasn't old and he'd already been successful. There were a few hardly-started letters of resignation angrily crumpled in the trash basket beside his desk in the den.

"I wish I could see. The big one just said, If I let you go will you promise to never .... I couldn't hear the rest. I wonder what he did. He got caught, didn't he, that's why he's crying. I swear to God I've never heard anyone cry like that before." Charlie pressed his nose to the screen. "Yes, he got caught," he added softly.

"What time is it," Sheila mumbled.

"I can't see the clock. The crying one said, Please, I'll just walk away if you'll let me, I'll just walk and won't ... won't something. He promised he wouldn't something."

The man's crying rose to screams. A car pulled up and stopped in the street, blocking Charlie's blurry view of the two people. The car left its lights on. "Please get out of the way," Charlie said.

"It's a cop," Sheila said. "And there's another."

There was a tangle of new voices. A few could be heard despite the screaming. Up against the car ... where's the baby? I'm the one that called you ... the baby's okay.

The screams became crying again, then moans.

"What's happening, what did he do? That big guy caught him, he wasn't hurt at all, imagine someone crying like that on the street outside our house."

"Tonight of all nights," Sheila murmured.

Charlie looked at her quickly. "I'm not afraid of what I have to do."

She didn't flinch. "Suit yourself."

He leaned his head against the screen. "Look at that—two more cop cars." He could see the flashing lights. "Who are they questioning by the car?"

"It's a woman."

"And they said something about a baby ... what could the guy have done? You know what? I don't think he's just a burglar."

"Okay, Sherlock."

"Maybe *you* don't care."

"Not at 2 a.m."

"Tell me when you'll be ready to start."

Sheila rolled away from the window, holding her pillow with her bare arms. She shut her eyes.

"The way he was crying—that's no thief ... the guy who caught him called him sick. I never heard anyone cry like that. He sounds like the *victim* , but ...."

Sheila turned to her back and looked at him. Her eyes were red-rimmed slits. All the voices outside had become softer. Charlie could neither see nor hear much. "You know what, Sheil, I'll bet that the crying guy lives next door to the big guy, and—you know how thin those apartment walls are over there— the big guy probably heard him beating the baby, that's what!"

"If you say so."

"Caught in the act."

"It sure makes confessing a lot easier."

"What's that supposed to mean?"

"Jesus, Charlie."

The dog stood up in its bed, circled, then lay down in a new position.

"Look at the damn dog," Charlie said. "Anyone comes to the door—she's all over the place barking, just a simple knock at the door. But someone's crying like the end of the world out in the street, and she doesn't even raise her goddamn ears. If it doesn't come through her front door, she doesn't give a shit."

"Smart dog." Sheila closed her eyes again and rolled to her

side. Charlie stared at her, then turned back to the window, his elbows on the sill, chin in his hands. Two of the police cars left. Cops were walking up and down the driveway. The big man and the woman were no longer in the street. The police radios were turned on high so the policemen could hear if any new crimes were being committed. The arrested man was a dark blur in the back seat of the first cop car—he whimpered once more. As Charlie got up to finish one of the letters, he wondered if the crying man would have just walked away if the other had let him go, or would he have walked away thinking about how he beat the baby.

Copterport on Cowell's Mountain

She's trying to pinpoint the truthful portions of a memory—because there must've been something more sensational. Didn't she surrender to him: *finally* give in and dash hysterically out the door, dancing and singing, into rain or snow or heavy traffic? Or was that someone else, somewhere else?

Eventually Stacey gets a part in the chorus of a summer musical a year after she quit her job as Tony Herald's all-purpose girl-friday. He stays in her mind like a tune. She's going back to see which quality of him was real, complete dauntlessness or listless apprehension. She seems to recall glimmers of genuine moments in between other times that might've never happened, probably didn't. Then why does she remember them?

Still, she's trying to remember correctly without letting any of it be distorted by the helplessness with which (she knows) it ended. She quit her transient job: she doesn't know why she feels the melancholy of deserting a passion.

He had given her a simple clerking position, and, so it seems, right from the beginning he audaciously pushed for her departure. Inevitable. She would go on to her true occupation.

In the meantime, and it started at the beginning, he often said, "What are you doing here?"

"You hired me, remember?"

"I didn't hire a singer."

Possibly the first time—yes, it seems during the first week—she answered, "I'll be a singer someday. Meanwhile I'll do this job."

"Do you know what *my* job really is?"

"You're a therapist."

"Actually I see other people's anxiety, see through them to the timidness which is in reality the biggest part of their lives. But luckily it's not a very contagious condition—timidness. You have to know a *carrier* in order to catch it."

"Are you worried about me being one?"

"Maybe."

It was August and her nose was peeling. His skin, despite sandy hair and lightly scattered freckles, pale eyes and white-blond eyebrows, was all over the same sunny brown.

"How will we ever know?" She smiled impishly, expecting the subject to drop. Expecting him to laugh gently, say "Ah, Stacey," and bend to sign his name to a patient's chart spread over his desk. Yes, in all certainty, that's where they were— that's where they always talked. He was seated in a plush office chair, and she would stand in front, on the other side of his desk, or sit in the chair reserved for the patient, having just been called from her own tiny table in the outer office. In between patients he often called her. Sometimes to sharpen pencils or to find something he'd lost, but always to talk.

But the subject *didn't* drop.

"*I* know." He looked up. She knows he was across the desk from her, she wishes she could remember if she ever touched him to make sure.

"*What* do you know?"

"I saw your résumé. You've been a waitress, an ice-cream store clerk, a typist in a pool, and a public relations gofer."

"I needed money."

"Yet these jobs have nothing to do with the *other* portions of your résumé: singing lessons, dancing classes, drama school.

Isn't—or *wasn't*—your intention to be some kind of enter-
tainer?"

"I guess. Yes. It still is."

"So I ask again, what're you doing *here*? Why aren't you out
there dancing and singing?"

There must've been a pause, she can't imagine answering
right away. She can't recall exactly what she did say—there's a
pause in the memory—but she can reconstruct her line by
working backwards from what he said afterwards. So she
might've said, "I'm not ready to audition."

He definitely said, "Oh? I think it's something different. I
think you're not ready to take a chance. Tell me if I'm wrong.
You're afraid to starve, to be uncomfortable for a while, to give
it everything you've got. Most of all, aren't you afraid to give up
your excuse of having to work and make money so you haven't
time to prepare for an audition. Am I right?"

She looked at him. She can guess what he saw: her mouth
felt small and pouty, her brow (she knew) creased in the middle,
her cheeks hot and probably pink. She looked out the window.
His office was six stories up.

The buzzer on his desk clicked, and the receptionist,
calmly from the outer office, reported that someone, a Mrs.
Something, was there. She was unexpected.

"She's usually suicidal," he said, and the woman entered,
burst in, flung herself into the room, shapeless in a Hawaiian
print dress—did she wear a necklace of flowers? She might've.
Probably not. Stacey must not've looked long; most of what she
remembers is the woman spread-eagle coming through the
door, spittle on her cheek and chin, fat hands, fat feet in sandals,
red polish on the nails of fingers and toes. But razor blades in her
hands? Blood at her throat? A gun? Poison? She might remember those. But probably not. She recalls him coming around
from behind the desk. To disarm the woman? Mostly she
remembers the word, *suicidal*, his fearless voice. She left the
room and shut the door.

He called to her later. After she'd already seen the Hawaiian-print woman leave the office, smile at the receptionist, exit softly, click the door shut gently. He called to her. He needed something. Couldn't find a pen or had no blank paper or needed a new incident report for the housewife's file. He needed something.

"Look at that mountain in the middle of the city." He was at the window, hands in pockets, undaunted, unwrinkled, hair still combed.

"That's not a mountain, it's a hill."

She must've helped him quickly, found whatever it was, tidied the office, (stood the furniture back upright?). She remembers clearly only the parts when she was standing still, watching him while they spoke.

"I like it, though, because there are no buildings or houses on it."

"Nor trees." She saw his profile as he looked out the window. She also saw the reflection, his face looking back in. His eyes were soft and unfocused, not watching with scrutiny for something hard to see or invisible. Not looking through anything. To his eyes, she knew, the glass had vanished.

"What's it called?" he asked.

"Cowell's Mountain."

"Ah ha! A mountain. I want to be up there. I'd like to live there, on the very top."

"Hard to come to work."

"Maybe I wouldn't." Perhaps she noticed, she thinks she did, his shoulders slacken, slump a little. He shut his eyes. "I'd sit at home and see over everyone's heads."

"Why?"

He looked at her. From Cowell's Mountain to her. She doesn't remember what she was wearing—she always wore pants and a shirt, and her hair was short.

"Well, for *one*, I wouldn't have to feel guilty about you."

"Then don't."

"You're bringing me coffee when you should be pursuing your calling. If it is one."

He sat on the edge of his desk. His smile so faint. She noticed that. She remembers, for certain, the smile which faltered a little. Very little.

"I'll buy you the top of that mountain," she said, "and put a copterport there so you can go home without climbing. When I get rich from my first real gig."

Then he was brash again and turned with a grin. "But you're not going to get anywhere *else* hanging around here. Go starve. It's a requirement."

"No, it's not. But being ready is."

She swears she doesn't know what she was waiting for. It might be what she's trying to remember. She keeps dreaming about him. Then why did she leave him?

She made him a fresh pot of coffee. He cupped his mug in two hands, closed his eyes, inhaling the sweet steam. He smiled up at her.

At first she wonders if maybe she shouldn't even try to remember the bravery stories, shouldn't bother to include them. Like whenever she retells herself the story of the old maintenance engineer in the building who stormed the outer office with a shotgun, holding the receptionist hostage, barrel pressed against the back of her neck, demanding that everyone leave. He was old and wanted to be alone with his building. He blew a hole in the ceiling and Tony Herald climbed through from the seventh floor to swiftly disarm the engineer. Afterward, the old man sobbed on Tony's shoulder. That whole story, in the end, always turns out to be a movie she'd seen, which had been adapted from a book.

Mostly the office was a little dull. He called her in for odd jobs. Sometimes he told her about a patient, how he calmly handled crisis and hysteria and didn't merely stay seated behind his desk. During these times, it seems she sees herself ın a different costume: a short skirt, a higher voice, hands folded on pressed-together knees, sensible heeled shoes. And one time he, with larger teeth in his grin, took out a sea captain's hat, set it gingerly on his head, smoothing it down in back. Stood next to his chair with one foot in the seat. He drank coffee from a beer stein. With gusto. He said, "Listen. This may inspire you. I was sailing my boat over to the island last weekend. The wind was north to south. Takes about five hours to get across, but we made it in three. We were drinking beer the whole way. There was no place to tie up, and we wanted dinner on the island, so we put the anchor down and swam ashore." He pushed the hat back on his head, his hair ruffled over his broad forehead. His dimples showed. She pressed her knees closer together and leaned forward.

"Later it was dark. My crew were all a little plastered—inexperienced drinkers. We got back to the beach and didn't see the boat. They panicked of course, too much root beer, and they started dashing back and forth, bumping into each other, jumping up and down, rolling around on the ground, wrestling, fighting, blaming each other, punching, squirming, some of them probably started to screw while they were down there. I wasn't watching them. While they groveled, I scanned the water. I have cat's eyes in the dark. I found the boat. It was pulling the anchor as it drifted."

Did she gasp? She might've. Raised her eyebrows, widened her eyes, a staring china doll.

"The anchor rope was tangled with two other boats' anchors, slowing it a little, but my boat had its mind set on reaching the rocks, so it pulled harder, taking the two other boats with it. All three at least 24-foot yachts. One of my crew had squeezed out of the wiggling crowd and was grasping my ankle. I shook my foot before diving into the water, but he came with me a little while, still holding my leg, then he dropped off. Maybe it was my wife, or maybe she was in a clench with one of the other guys on the sand. While they shouted and snorted on the beach, I had to go get the boat. Insurance is skyrocketing. I went under and found the anchor rope."

"Wasn't it dark?" Her voice piped like a flute.

"Very. But I had to see—no excuses would save the boat. I took the rope and swam backwards, pulling the boats, all three of them. The rope slithered in my hands, trying to get away. All three boats fought and splashed like hooked marlin, spinning, trying to get to the rocks where they could saw through the ropes and get away."

"Did you make it?"

"Of course." He smiled. "You see, someone had to get into the water and just do what was necessary to save the boat. Someone had to see clearly enough, calmly enough over the heads of everyone who panics and freezes or struggles."

"And you were the one."

"I'm always the one."

She thinks hard, trying to remember how she managed the quick-change in an off-stage wing to get back into her pants and shirt and shoes with laces. He, without the captain's hat, seemed smaller sitting behind the desk. He propped his head up with a fist on his cheek, which nearly closed one eye. Still, he looked at her, with all of one eye and some of the other. "That's what I do around here, you know." He glanced out the window, toward Cowell's Mountain—a small, lazy propeller plane circling the peak. "Think you can quit yet?"

"Not yet." She tap-danced out the door with the empty coffee pot.

For another story, she thinks she wore a checkered pinafore over a white blouse, very short, her petticoat almost showed. Her nails had grown, especially while listening to the story, and she painted them with rose polish to match the rose blush on her cheeks. Her nylons were sheer, her legs trim, her sandals were Italian leather with little heels. She carried a white patent leather purse with a gold chain. She sat and crossed her ankles only. She served him tea and cookies on his oak desk. She wet her lips and he began: "I was getting married the next day. I was driving somewhere in my old convertible sports car."

His hands were steady. He took a cookie without spilling any powdered sugar from the top. He bit and no crumbs fell. "I'm still not sure what happened, it probably doesn't even matter. Someone made a left turn in front of me, I think, as I went through an intersection, someone jumped the curb and came at me, gunning for me, a demolition-derby car with a number 76 on the side. That was the year, also the month and day of the wedding. Probably one of her old boyfriends." His hands were not nervous and he didn't touch himself anywhere. He barely moved. His mouth told the story.

"When he hit me, my car rolled over. I'm not sure how many times. I tumbled through the intersection, end over end, made a left, still rolling, slowed and rolled into a driveway. It was my wife's mother's house. I woke up on the front lawn."

"Were you hurt?" she breathed.

He stood up for the scar at the end of the show. "My car was flat. Even the wheels, flat. It was upside-down in their rose garden. One tire on the roof. One tire caught on my foot. I still had the steering wheel when they found me. See this?" He began to roll up his pant leg but couldn't roll it far enough, so he took a knife from his desk drawer and slit the pants, tore them to his crotch. His thigh flexed, tight muscles like cables rose under his skin. The whole thigh was blue. "Fifteen years ago, maybe close to twenty, and still bruised. You should've seen it then. Go ahead, touch it."

Like wide bands of steel under his blue skin. He sat down and began to sew his pants. He had the needle and thread on a cardboard in his shirt pocket. He had to remove her hand twice.

"I still got married. I got up and said, let's go! It was the wedding day. Everyone was crying, but I was laughing and said, Look! I did jumping jacks for them, and push-ups and sit-ups. I ran a mile. My wife sobbed, You've ruined the honeymoon. But I hadn't. I came through."

Stacey clasped her hands under her chin.

She stood to clean the desk, pick up the cookie tray, tea pot and china mugs. He spilled his last cup. "Whoops!" The coffee trickled off the desk and onto her pants, but it was okay because they were brown anyway.

"So whadda'ya think? Get the message?"

"I think so."

"Go ahead, crash, get it over with. It won't be fatal."

She punched out the bottom of his paper cup, made it into a glider and sailed it out the window.

She seems to definitely recall her costume for the last story he told, although she doesn't think she ever owned such a thing. A pure white nightshirt dress, tied at the waist with a white cord. She doesn't remember any shoes. She may've been barefoot. It was simple, and she wasn't made up at all. Her face was early morning pale. She doesn't think she was actually tired. The story brought back bloom to her cheeks.

"There was a code green in this mental hospital where I worked— that means someone went nuts." He sat on top of his desk, leaned his back against the window glass, drew his knees up and circled them with his arms. "It was three a.m. Some kid decided to go home. A big kid. He was walking down the hall with a chess game balanced on a board, all set up and half played. I was the only man on the staff that night. I locked all the nurses in the ward at the end. I could see them through the tiny window in the door, about fifty of them squirming and wiggling behind the door, jousting to get their faces in the window. I still remember it clearly, when one was looking through the window, another would put her hand on top of the first one's head and push her under like dunking her in water. They pounded on the door. Yelled like murder."

"People are always milling around hysterically ·in your stories."

"That's how people are. I saw the guy way up the hall, at the other end, backed up against the locked door there. All the doors were locked. Just he and I were in a long hall. The nurses booed. He was sitting on the floor, back against the door, sucking each of the chess pieces, then tossing them away. Know what I did?"

"No."

"I let him out."

"Huh?"

"See, all those nurses were frantic about a committed patient getting away, all the implications and punishment, news articles, blame, revenge, reprisals. They were crazy. Out of their minds. But I knew he'd be back the next day. They cackled like hens at me all night. Tied me to a chair and surrounded me, chattered at me and told me stories about the vile punishments I would get in the hospital employees' union hall torture chamber. In the morning, there he was, waiting at the door with a chess board. He might've never gone off the front porch all night. See, I had thought clearly and made a rational decision and wasn't preoccupied with thoughts of death."

He stretched. His forearms flexed to twice their size. He leaped from the desk and landed lightly on his toes. He twirled like an ice dancer until he was a vertical blur, and stopped, without slowing first, facing the window and Cowell's Mountain.

"I'm not succeeding, am I?" he said.

"I've listened to every word." But now it was just getting interesting. She rubbed her saddle shoes against the rug, stood and straightened her jeans. She seems to think there might've been a rule about not wearing denim. Perhaps it was her rule. It was unlikely that he ever told her what to wear in his office.

"But I'm not succeeding."

"With what?"

"You." He turned from the window. "Making you tough enough."

"I just can't leave until I'm ready." She'd been there over a year. Heard many more stories than she can now call to mind.

He looked at her, gazed at her, stared through her, passed his eyes swiftly over, looked at her a long while. Then back out the window. "You have an awful strong weakness."

She was still. She watched his back. Watched him the same way she thinks she'd watched him during each story, the way she remembers concentrating, carefully sorting details, waiting for the clues. But that time—as though finally there was something obvious enough for her to catch—his back flinched. He rested his forehead against the window glass. Just for a second.

She touched his coat. "Don't worry. Someday I'll be successful and rich and you can retire from saving lives 'cause I'll buy you the top of Cowell's Mountain. You can sit and watch the sun set over everyone's floundering heads."

He turned. His pale eyes almost lost inside his sockets. Yellow-leather skin. Crow's feet at his eyes and sweat on his brow. He passed a hand across his mouth. It may as well be a photograph, as many times as this sight has been called for retrospect.

"Bring me my tape recorder, then go home."

It was the next day, Friday, nearly five, when he finally called her in again. He was watching the sun lower itself over the ocean. Everything in the view was growing shadows. Except the western side of Cowell's Mountain which stood upright to face the sun almost directly. It was still midday there.

"I have something for you," he said. From his leather coat pocket he took a cassette tape. She didn't hesitate, like in movies, watching his eyes in either bewilderment or tenderness, making him continue to hold the tape out to her. She took it and checked the label. Nothing written there. When she looked up, he was pushing a large glass jar at her across the desk. "And this. It has special meaning for me because of the time it was given to me. I'm sure I told you the story. Now I'm giving it to you."

It actually wasn't a jar. She of course knows that now (no need to remember) because it still sits on her bedroom shelf. It's a beer mug, clear glass, one-half gallon, printing on the side: *I Bet You Can't.*

He leaned across the desk to put his eyes on the same axis as hers, so he wasn't looking up from under his brows nor glancing down his cheeks at her. She remembers well those dull pewter eyes. "You've been here over a year, and I've never taken the time to do this."

"What?"

"Go listen to the tape. Go home. Get comfortable. Don't do anything else. Just listen. Go on."

So she lay on her bed and pushed the tape into her little recorder, held the mug on her stomach, reading it while looking through it to her wall of theater posters and movie advertisements.

"Actually, Stacey," he began. The voice was gruff. Possibly a cheap tape, or poor play-back. "Time wasn't the reason I was never completely straight with you. A person always has time." She doesn't need to remember: preserved on tape, it can't be considered unreliable remembrance. This is memorization, line by line, his words, a tinny voice on synthetic tape, more real than reminiscence. She's never had to wonder, *Is it really you?*

"Ah Stacey, you're afraid, but not of the right thing. You *should* be afraid of your own weakness which may prevent you from taking action to pursue your mission. Trying to get you to quit wasn't a game to me. All these months I've tried to be an example of personal fortitude. And when it comes down to the bottom line, none of it really mattered to you. You listened and listened, and then you only saw the *real* me. Seeing through people makes me tired. I love my job, but it makes me tired. I wouldn't mind quitting and renting out my boat, being a charter captain for tourists. You saw it, you must've, because finally instead of responding with bizarre gawking admiration, you showed both intelligence and emotion. I don't want you serving me coffee anymore, sharpening my pencils, keeping me organized. You'll be happier, I know it, doing what you... *should* ... want to do. I—" The voice broke. He cleared his throat. She has run back and forth over this inch of tape thousands of times. He coughed again, lightly. She smiled softly and listened with gentle confidence. His voice began again: "I know I told you how calm I am when people are hysterical—how cool I always was in making all the decisions and acting on them. Well, it's inevitable, someday I'm not gonna do it—everyone'll be disappointed. Or maybe dead. Just like you're afraid to try, I can't ever let down and *stop*. I've never told anyone else. I'm glad ... also sorry... I told you." His voice wobbled. The tape could've been warped. But it wasn't. She checked once. The faltering voice gave her something to stand on, an oddly realistic comfort. She heard him breathe deeply, exhale slowly. He waited. Then stopped the tape.

She quit after that. This part she knows. This is authentic.

He came into the office on Monday, stooped, thinner. He didn't stop in the reception area. He closed the door of his office quickly. Stacey followed, without being called, entered without knocking. He was seated, looking down at the bare top of his desk where he'd flattened his hands, palms down. His knuckles were skinned, bruised. There were stitches across one thumb, curving around toward the underside. Bruises splotched at intervals up his arms. One cheek was scraped raw. His eyelids were red, puffy, half closed. "I had an accident with the boat," he said. "We almost lost it."

"But you didn't."

"No."

"I'm giving two weeks notice."

"I know." He closed his eyes. He held his temples in his fingertips.

She was still standing just inside the closed door. She never stepped forward. Not even when he sat up and said, "I hurt all over." He pressed a hand against his ribs. His mouth turned down at the corners. "I want you to stay."

"You mean until the first of the month?"

"No, I want you to stay. I don't want you to quit." He leaned on the desk again. "I shouldn't have said that. I never would have, except I'm so sore."

She smiled and was able to say, "I'm leaving anyway."

"I know. I'm glad."

He didn't reach out to her, and they never shook hands.

What seems like the bare bones of something that happened is actually everything that happened.

She never wrote a letter of resignation, but a year later finally knows what to say. She talks back to the tape, after his voice is finished, she says into the machine, I kept thinking I was impressed by someone's strength, but now realize I was only waiting—hoping—to see weakness. I was just the opposite of you."

Then she leaves the playbill—where her tiny part doesn't even have a name—with the receptionist to give to him later. She'll never be able to buy him his heliport.

Bad Luck with Cats

She was half dressed, wearing black underwear and one of Jerry's undershirts, when someone she didn't know knocked on the door. "Do you have a black and white cat?" the someone asked.

"Jerry, stay *here*," she called over her shoulder as she ran on her toes down the front walk.

He was already in the doorway. "What?"

"Get back inside!" She scooped up the mess in the street with one hand. One eye was dangling out of its socket.

"Brenda, what're you doing?" he shouted from the front yard.

"Go away, get back!" Trying to hide the cat's body, she rolled it up in the bottom part of her undershirt. A bloody papoose against her stomach. He was coming toward her, so she made a wide circle around him, running over some finely crushed glass in the street, then down the alley to the first trashcan she could find. There was a blot of blood on the front of her shirt. She dropped the undershirt in the trash on top of the cat then held an empty box over her chest as she jumped the back fence and went in through the back door. A few nights back she'd had a dream about going to a symphony concert without a shirt on. She thought, *so this's what THAT was all about*.

"Jerry, you here?" He didn't answer. She left the box by the door and went into the bedroom, scooting quickly past the still-open front door.

Jerry was on the bed, lying diagonally like he had the last time, his face turned away from her. "Honey? Jerry?"

"It was Ozzie, wasn't it?"

"Yes."

"You don't even care."

"Don't say that."

"Well, you don't."

"Don't start it again." She took out another one of his undershirts.

"Like clockwork," he said. "Every six months."

"It was almost a year ago."

In a way, though, he was right—it was only six months since he'd stopped mourning for Mikey, the dumb one, found stone dead in the gutter, not a mark on his body. Just too damn dumb to get out of the street. She hadn't been home. Jerry had carried Mikey to the porch, then went to a neighbor and asked what he should do next. He saved his crying until she got home and he confessed that Mikey had been pestering him while he was practicing the xylophone, so he'd put the cat out, probably just twenty minutes before it happened. But he'd stopped crying and closed himself in his music room for several hours when he found out she'd thrown Mikey away instead of burying him. At least when they lost Big Sam, there was no evidence—he'd just stopped coming home one night.

She thought *It's getting messier every time.*

Jerry rolled over. He was wearing a T-shirt with a picture of Bobby Fischer on the front. Brenda got the penny jar from the dresser and poured a pile onto the mattress, then kneeled on the floor and started counting out sets of fifty.

"I think we'd better go through with it," Jerry said.

"With what?"

"You know."

"I don't think this is a good time to talk about it." She found a slug among the coins and swore under her breath. Every time a cat died, he asked for a divorce.

"Where are Bessie and Spunky?" he asked.

"Around."

"Do you think they miss Ozzie? Think they saw it happen?"

"Come on, Jerry." She shook her head and began stacking the pennies into wrappers from the bank.

"You're right, what a stupid thing to say. I thought I would someday grow up and get over this kind of stuff. But, *no*."

"You're too old to grow up any more." She smiled at him.

"Yeah. So how'm I gonna be able to suddenly become a pizza delivery boy or sell popcorn at the movies?"

"*How* to do it is simple—you just *do* it." She had three dollars in pennies wrapped, so she put the remaining coins back into the jar. "Besides, the symphony isn't folding—it's just a strike."

"*I'm* not striking," he said. "Anyway, we've got to figure out what to do with Bessie and Spunky."

"Why?"

"This is a crummy place for cats."

"So what do you suggest?"

"We could move."

"You kidding? Eventually, yes. But *now*? Just for the cats?"

"Then let *me* move."

"*Let* you? Who's stopping you? I just think it's a dumb idea."

"I know. Aren't all my ideas dumb?"

"Hey," she said. "Want to walk up to the store with me? I've got to get some milk and cereal."

"No. I'm going to find Spunky and Bessie and keep them inside until I think of what to do with them."

When Brenda came back, he told her he'd arranged to give the two remaining cats to a friend's father who had a small farm off the old highway that snaked through the Indian reservation. They would deliver the cats to the friend at the union hall after the meeting that night, and the friend would take them to his father. So Jerry was keeping the cats inside until it was time to go. The cats sat at the front door, looking over their shoulders and crying, standing up on their hind legs and sniffing the keyhole, digging their claws into the carpet under the doorway until Brenda shouted at them. She and Jerry were sitting at the kitchen table deciding what he could do during the work stoppage.

"It won't last forever," she said. "You could find something temporary."

"It's *already* been forever. Why is our union doing this to us? We'll end up playing for every rinky-dink road show or circus that comes through and needs back-up music for a clown graduation or trained dogs. That's just as bad as forever."

She had two blank pieces of paper to write down all the ideas they came up with. One list was for things he could do, the other was for her. Her list was already started: *piano lessons*. The paper was stationery from one of the schools where she substituted, but the teachers didn't seem to get sick very often. "Okay, let's get serious," she said. "How about ... we could go to the park and perform duets with a donation hat."

"A voice and percussion duet? Great."

"Just kidding. But remember how I sang at the park with my brother shaking a tambourine—we made a bundle."

"Yeah," Jerry said. "Ten dollars in half a day—"

"We're not accomplishing anything," she said. It started to rain. The cats had finally gone to sleep on the sofa, but raised their heads when the rain began to hit the metal rain gutter.

"Hey," she said. "Whadda you say to forgetting all this for a while and going into the bedroom?"

"*Now*? Ozzie just got killed this morning."

"And tomorrow he'll have just been killed yesterday, and the next day he'll have just been killed the day before yesterday...."

"What's that supposed to mean?"

Brenda shrugged. "Forget it." The downpour suddenly intensified, as though someone outside had turned a hose onto the front window. "Wow, lookit that. Do we *have* to go to that meeting?"

"*I* have to," he said. "Greg's meeting me to pick up the cats."

One of the cats stretched, hopped off the sofa and came toward the table, purring, then jumped into Jerry's lap. "I have something to admit," Jerry said.

After Brenda wrote *secretary* on her list, she folded her hands on the tabletop, smiling slightly at him.

"Why're you looking at me like that?"

"Just waiting for what terrible thing you're going to 'fess up to," she said. "I can hardly wait. As a matter of fact, though, sometimes I wish you'd hit me or go gamble away all our money—what's left of it—or get into some really vicious drugs and start hocking stuff, or maybe start fucking around, or... I don't know, something really *bad*."

"Why?"

"Because, Jerry, what could we possibly say to a lawyer? That we're incompatible because there're no duets written for voice and percussion? Or that life is intolerable because you need help starting the lawn mower or using a Phillips screwdriver? Or that I can't respect you as a man because you watch the same movies over and over and still get all misty-eyed?"

"Is that true?"

" That's not what I'm saying. That's not the point. It's just that we don't have anything *bad* enough to say."

"That's bad enough."

"Are you kidding—isn't a man in the 80's supposed to be *sensitive*? Okay, go on and finish admitting, then we'll have to get going," she said. "Maybe I'll admit something too."

Jerry looked down at the cat. He was holding his hand very rigidly in a fist so the cat could rub its head against his knuckles. "It was my fault ... again."

"It's no one's fault. It happens."

"It didn't have to happen. Last night when I went to put them in the shed, I couldn't catch Ozzie. He kept playing with me, hiding under the car, racing around me. So I said, okay, if you want to stay out all night, be my guest."

"So you think you're a jinx and no cat is safe around you?"

"Why d'you have to say stuff like that?"

"Why d'you tell me stuff like that? What am I *supposed* to say?"

He looked up briefly, then continued watching the cat butt its head against his knuckles. "Maybe you could say nothing. You could sit there and listen. You don't *have* to answer if you're not going to say anything helpful or the least bit ... sympathetic."

"That would be fine, if you ever talked about anything that mattered."

"What if the things I choose to talk about matter to me?"

"You know what, Jerry?" she grinned. "You should've been a soap opera star. I swear, eighty percent of the women in America would be in love with you."

"Great. The one I'm married to doesn't even watch TV."

"Okay, how about this?" She chuckled while writing *movie star* on his piece of paper, then passed the paper across the table to him. "So ... you feel guilty about Ozzie. Okay, I'll sit here and listen. Really, I'm listening." She bent to write *housekeeper* and *gardener* on her list.

"Sure."

"Really. How d'you feel guilty?"

"Well ... they depend on me. I let them down. I guess I let you down too."

"No you didn't." She got up and went into the bedroom to get their raincoats.

"Yes I did. I *had* to be a musician, didn't I. Now lookit the mess we're in."

"No you didn't." She smiled and handed him the car keys. "I never depended on you."

"Good thing. Who would? I don't do anything useful."

"Jerry, look, just listen: You're like the cats. You have to do the thing that makes you what you are. Just like they *had* to do the things that being a cat is all about—so they got squashed." She went back to her list and wrote *truck driver, child care,* and *sex.*

"No," Jerry said. "You can't convince me that being a cat automatically includes getting hit by cars."

"Okay." She crossed out *sex*.

"Let's *go*." He grabbed her list, crumpled it and tossed it into the kitchen sink.

The meeting was supposed to be private, for union members only, but Brenda stood in the doorway and listened to someone recite a list of laughable items on the latest offer from management. Almost everyone in the room did at least chuckle after each item, so sometimes she missed the first few words of the next one. But Jerry wasn't laughing. He was sitting in the back row on the opposite side of the room from where Brenda was huddled in the doorway. It was still raining and the roof had a very small awning. When the wind came up, the rain slanted and doused not only the porch but the floor inside the room too, so it wasn't as though she was dry, just drier than she would be standing in the parking lot.

Jerry had asked her why the hell she wanted to come. He was sitting there with one elbow on one knee, his cheek in his hand. It was the same way he'd sat in his classes fifteen years ago at college. He was really almost exactly the same as when she was first attracted by his graceful walk, his easy laugh. He'd even been a campus hero for a week in 1971 after his ingenious efforts in a psychological test and interview had succeeded in getting him out of the draft. He'd received the *unfit* designation he'd sought—the poor duped analyst had diagnosed him *neurotically immature* and had suggested treatment. It kept him out of the draft but he couldn't avoid ROTC. Back then in Missouri, every boy had to take two years of ROTC, so Jerry had protested by getting D's. It wasn't as easy as it sounded. He had to be precise to make sure they *were* D's and not F's. He wouldn't want to have to repeat ROTC. He'd marched with a snare drum in the ROTC band. Brenda suddenly remembered he'd learned how to take a gun apart and put it back together.

A gust of wind suddenly spattered the rain across her back. She'd missed the last several items while thinking about ancient history. The list of management's offers had moved on from compensation to working conditions, and management's latest proposed language concerning the backstage area had removed *suitable* from the old contract's wording: *Each musician shall have a suitable locker*. The rain intensified, hitting the pavement in the parking lot with a sound like water on a hot griddle, so someone got up and closed the door and Brenda had to run back to the car for shelter.

They were parked next to the guy who was taking the cats to his father's dirt-farm. The cats were in a big cardboard box on the guy's back seat. The box was no longer rocking, so the cats had probably settled down. She sat tapping her foot, twisting her hair, pushing her cuticles back, staring at the rivulets running down the windshield.

She tried to get him up at nine and again at ten, but he didn't stagger into the bathroom until eleven-thirty. "You're still here," he said after his shower. "Didn't you get any calls?"

"No one's sick today. You missed the rally, you know, you slept right through."

"You thought I should go do that teamster stuff?"

"I was going to go with you."

"What the hell for?"

"I like to watch you picket," she said. "You look so ...."

"So much like a guy who's picketing."

"No, you look so ... different somehow."

"Maybe you just never saw a bunch of assholes walking in circles holding signs."

It was no longer raining. The sun had been out since the

clouds broke at around seven that morning when she'd gotten up to make apple sauce out of the box of bruised apples she'd bought at a farmer's market for $2. The last of the jars was being processed at noon. Every window was steamed-up and the house smelled appley. Jerry was reading the paper, but he'd discarded the classified ads. She was going to spread the ads out and go through them to see what jobs they could go apply for, but the phone rang. It was too late to get a substituting job that day, and too early to be an assignment for tomorrow. Jerry didn't move, so after four rings, Brenda picked it up. It was the guy who'd taken the cats to his father. She stood leaning against the wall in the kitchen where she could see Jerry still looking at the sports page, and she listened to the guy explaining how his father had put the box in an empty horse stall and opened it, but didn't take the cats out because it's best to let them explore new territory on their own. But, he assumed, something had frightened them—maybe one of the cats who already lived there, or one of about twenty dogs his father kept— so Bessie and Spunky had left the box a lot sooner than he would've expected them to *want* to leave. Maybe the thunder and lightning had frightened them too, and since they didn't know where they were, they didn't know where to go, and the bottom line was they'd just flat-out disappeared. Maybe they would come back, the guy said, but with all that rain, his father wasn't holding out too much hope. That was an awful lot of rain, the guy said. It was just too much rain.

Brenda thanked the guy and hung up. Jerry didn't even ask *what was that?* like he usually did after she got a phone call. She went back to where she'd spread the classified ads on the floor, kneeled, read down one column and asked, "Is busboy or hospital orderly okay?"

"Oh god, I guess so," he groaned. He had a page folded to the crossword puzzle, then began rhythmically stabbing his pencil through the paper.

Then she told him about Bessie and Spunky. "They could be hiding, Jerry. They might just suddenly come out from underneath something and go ask for something to eat. Or they may even find their way back *here*. It's happened, hasn't it?"

"In Disney movies." He got up and went into the bedroom. She sighed, paused for a second staring at an opening for a dishwasher, then followed him, but he wasn't lying across the bed nor looking up divorce lawyers in the phone book. He was in the closet, kneeling, with his head hidden underneath the clothes. When he backed out, he had his leather high top sneakers.

"What's up?" she said. "You gonna wear those for picketing tomorrow? Your bad ankle bothering you?"

"Hell no. I'm going out to look for the cats."

"*Now?*"

"Tomorrow morning, if they don't come out this afternoon like you said."

"You mean, we're gonna search that whole valley out there?"

"*You* don't have to come."

"Who's gonna carry you home when you step on a wasp's nest or trip in a gopher hole or slip in the mud?" She stopped and sniffed. "I think the applesauce is done."

"I hate it when you get this way," he said.

"What way?"

"Rushing all over *doing* stuff." He sat on the bed holding the shoes, one on each knee. They were still almost new. She'd convinced him to buy them after his last bad ankle sprain two years before. He looked at her. "You ready to admit it yet?"

"What're you talking about?"

"Why'd it have to rain, anyway," he groaned. "I *hate* rain."

"It needs to rain or things won't grow."

He left his shoes on the bed and went back to the living room, stepped on the classified ads on his way to the sofa, and picked up the tattered crossword puzzle. Brenda went out into the backyard to weed the small garden area she'd cleared the week before. She'd planted some quick-growing, easy-care vegetables—lettuce, chard, bush beans, green pepper. The ground was saturated and the small plants were flattened. She used twigs to support the ones the weren't beaten to death. There was snake on the lawn that she killed with the hoe.

It wasn't really a farm at all. It was about 50 square yards where the sagebrush had been cleared, surrounded by a low, leaning chain-link fence to keep the pack of dogs from roaming free. The house was a converted portable horse stall. The barn was several more portable horse stalls, facing each other with sheet metal covering the space between the roofs. There were two sheep in a pen, their dirty wool full of burrs and sticks. There were a few chickens loose with the dogs. There were three horses in stalls, one empty stall where the feed was stored, one stall used as a pen for some puppies. A few cats sat on the roof and on the gates of the stalls. There hadn't been any other houses on the last three miles of dirt road. The telephone wires stopped where the paved road did. The guy had a generator for power and a tank to hold water.

"A great place to be a cat," Brenda said, "but a lousy place to be a person. Dust and stickers. I'm not against *dirt*, but … it turns into mud."

"Great place to be a cat if you're not chased away by all the dogs."

"Or eaten by a coyote," she said, which she hadn't said before, although she knew it must've occurred to him. Sure enough, he turned sharply and said, "Shut up."

The owner of the place wasn't there, but his son had said to go on up and look around for the cats. The dogs barked but let them come through the gate. Jerry had brought a cat toy—a plastic ball with a bell inside—which he shook in one hand as he walked through the makeshift barn and called the cats' names.

They looked under every feed sack, behind every bale of hay, between boxes of tools and horse junk. Then they walked around the inside perimeter of the fence, looking under abandoned pieces of sheet metal, peering into dark holes in an old water tank. There was another opening in the fence—not a gate, just a place where two ends of the chain link came together and were tied shut with a piece of rope. Jerry untied the knot.

"Where're you going?" she asked.

"I'm searching for the cats, what did you think I was going to do out here, look for a *job*?"

"I don't know which would be more impossible."

There was an erosion path winding down into a shallow canyon. The dirt was still wet but the day was probably 85 degrees and there were no trees and no shade. The ground practically gave off visible steam. The highest bushes came only to their waists. The little trail was rutted down the middle. It was also filled with holes of various sizes—big enough for a squirrel or skunk, small enough for a spider or wasp.

"What makes you think the cats would stay on a trail?" she asked.

"You have a better idea?"

After a moment she said, "I guess not." Then added, "But how do you know how far to go, and how do you know when you've gone far enough?"

Jerry didn't answer. He paused every few steps to shake the toy and call the cats' names. Once his foot hit some slimy mud and slid out from underneath him, but he caught himself with his palms against some big rocks, then went on calling, pausing to scan the area, moving on again.

They'd gone down the trail far enough so they couldn't see the barn anymore, but a view was opening in front of them. Their shallow canyon was only a side entry into a huge basin, surrounded by other tributary canyons and even more rounded rolling hills: *all* of them, hill and dale, equipped uniformly with a sea of dry scrubby bushes growing over last year's mat of flattened gray grass; an abundance of holes and cracks and fissures and crevices; an assortment of rocks small enough to throw, graduating up to big enough to rise like islands or jut out like mini lookout cliffs; and all of it slathered—for now—in mud. The whole unvarying terrain went on forever, without a tree or river to break the sameness or provide a goal. They would never be able to cover it all foot-by-foot, shaking every clump of brush, jingling the cat toy outside every dark cleft between two rocks, kicking every bush, following every erosion trail, rolling every boulder. And even if they could eventually cover it all, could actually look *everywhere*, they'd never find *anything*. While they were looking here, Bessie could be torn in half and eaten by a coyote three miles away, the carcass filled with maggots, the head carried down a hole by a possum or skunk, and the pieces scattered by crows and buzzards. By the time Jerry worked his way three miles to the west or east or south or wherever she'd been killed, there'd be nothing there. He'd just step right over the mound of red ants swarming over a piece of her tail and go on looking. Things *could* just disappear, no longer exist—why go on sweating in flaming sun and sliding around in sticky mud and getting clawed by tumbleweed thorns trying to find something that's just not *there* anymore?

"Oh god, Jerry, it's *hopeless!*"

He was about ten steps in front of her. She sat on a flat rock which was flush with the ground, the bushes towering over her head. "What're we gonna *do*, what'll we *do*?" She was screaming and Jerry was slipping in the mud, coming back up the trail toward her. "Look at us, look at us, we're thirty-five and we don't have jobs! We just can't go on like this—how *can* we?"

Jerry squatted beside her then crouched over her, hugging her with his arms and legs. Her nose was in his ear and her mouth open against his jaw. He ran his hand down her spine then softly patted the back of her head. "We can't, we can't, we can't," she moaned. "And what difference does it make? What's gonna change if we go on for another five minutes or another six months?"

She almost fell over into the mud as Jerry pushed away and stood up. She stared as he wiped her tears off his cheek and neck, his eyes slits, then he went back down the trail, calling the cats and shaking the toy. She watched until he was out of sight and she couldn't even hear him anymore.

Laying Off the Secretary

What're you gonna do with her when you don't really need her anymore? Needing to trim the fat doesn't always mean it's hog butchering time.

At the farm's budget meeting, Hal, Director of Farming, announces that he's over-staffed. Hal has recently married his friend Jack's sister and has returned from his honeymoon the day of the budget meeting, where he sits four chairs away from Jack, newly hired Breeding Consultant. Just before his honeymoon, with Jack's help, Hal had reorganized and redistributed all farm responsibilities, allowing employees to concentrate on their specialties and creating new positions. Now what? Should the harvest squad also have to pull weeds? Should those who shovel manure also feed the cows? Should the egg-counter also count chickens? They could replace several people with trained dogs, but someone has to train and take care of the dogs.

Of course there's no question about the value of and need for the Associate Farming Director and the Assistant Farming Director. These modern-day farms with their business managers, accountants, and secretaries ... but why couldn't the brand new farmer's-wife do something useful? That's what they decide. So the secretary can be omitted.

The secretary isn't present to take notes during these private meetings, but afterwards they'll have her type up the new budget proposal. It's common knowledge that she won't even read what she's typing, won't notice she's been eliminated;

Cris Mazza

she'll have no comment, make no alternate suggestions. She is a pure and professional secretary. Too bad, because that would be an easy way to notify her.

It's Hal's job to hire and fire. Experience has taught him that he has to be sensitive. "No one knows how difficult it is to fire someone," he says. Jack nods. They are in the inner executive office, but the door is wide open between the two offices. In the outer office, the secretary is doing whatever it is she does all day.

"Especially when it's someone who never blinks," Hal adds.

"I haven't heard her speak yet," says Jack.

"She also never laughs."

"And never eats."

"Never goes to the bathroom."

"Never breathes?"

"Never has an expression."

Jack glances into the outer office. "Can we assume she does or will, while we're somewhere else?"

"I don't see how we can."

The phone rings once. The secretary must've answered it, but they can't hear her voice.

"We should have another meeting," Hal says, "to figure out how to do this." He checks the schedules of the Associate and Assistant Farm Directors. The only time they're all on duty together is at feeding time, two hours a day when the whole farm works in harmony. No meetings can be scheduled then. Hal will be standing on a raised platform to oversee—hearing the farm's sounds, smelling the farm's smells.

He sighs. "It's easier to seduce someone than to fire them. Then it's easier to kick them out of bed than fire them. Inciting and discontinuing a sexual relationship with her would ultimately be easier to do than tell her she will no longer be what she's always been."

Jack is hanging photos over his new desk—the ancestry of his championship sheep.

"So screw her, *then* fire her."

"I'm a married man."

It's not the secretary who is humming in the background—that's the electric typewriter.

Jack says, "Okay, then promote her. Give her another job."

"She's a *secretary*."

"Change what she is. Put her in charge of trees and tell her to leave. Make her the egg inspector and tell her to beat it. Put her in charge of the ducks and tell her to get-the-flock-out-of-here."

There *are* other jobs needing to be filled. A position on the equipment crew for a specialist in lawn mowers. A milking-machine expert. A breeding manager for the horses. Also a few other positions, but those require trained experts. The secretary is summoned. "You're now on Jack's staff, manager of the horse-breeding. Congratulations," Hal says, extending a hand which remains extended without being joined in a handshake.

Jack explains: There are two studs, one younger, one more experienced. The experienced stud should only be paired with mares from outside his bloodline; the younger one—the white one—can be paired with daughters and granddaughters of the old stud, unless the mares are black or pinto, in which case they should be paired with a loaner-stud from upstate because last year the younger stud caused two horribly freckled foals out of a black and a pinto mare, so that has to be avoided. The objective this year is more broad-chested foals without terribly long legs nor high hips. This isn't a thoroughbred breeding farm, these are work animals, also for sale to riding stables. The horses should be paired to enhance the necessary good qualities: gentleness, strong legs, attractive coats, sturdy backs, lots of heart.

The secretary handles this information as inter-office communication and files it.

With a good breeding season, Jack could look for promotion to Second-Assistant Farming Director. In a week Hal and Jack inspect the breeding stock. The mares are in their pasture. The studs are each in their separate pastures. The secretary is sitting on a fence post between the two studs.

"What's going on here?" Hal asks.

The secretary is handling correspondence and clerical work for the number-one stud.

"What has he sent?" Hal asks Jack.

Jack checks into it. "Not even a love letter."

Hal has too many other pressing worries. (As usual, the Associate and Assistant Directors are fighting over jurisdiction of the senior harvest unit.)

Breeding time passes; all the stud's correspondence is filed. Meanwhile the younger stud, ignored and frustrated, breaks down the bars and ruts six black-and-white mares.

What a mess.

Now Hal has to turn his attention away from his feuding assistants and tend to the horses. He is clever and solves both problems by putting the Assistant Farming Director in charge of finding a new manager of horse-breeding, and assigns the Associate Director the special task of selling the impregnated mares and buying new breeding stock, preferably this time just plain-old brown.

The secretary is back in the outer office where secretaries belong.

"What now?" Hal asks Jack. Can she bucket-train the calves? Can she prune the plum trees? Can she handle general pest control? Does Jack need an assistant somewhere else, maybe in the barn?

"No!" Jack is worried that the secretary has already hurt his possible promotion.

"I'll think of something," Hal says. Since Jack is in between breeding projects, Hal sends him to find out how the Assistant and Associate Farming Directors are doing, which Jack is more than pleased to do because spying on the Associate Director and reporting back to the Director certainly can't hurt his status. Hal is aware of Jack's ambition. An ambitious man is valuable until his ambitions aim him toward the position of the person he is valuable to. But there was really no need for Hal to send Jack to check the Assistant and Associate; if they don't do their jobs, Hal will know. It isn't easy to hide six pregnant pinto horses. And it doesn't really matter how much they grumble while working, which is all Jack will be able to report: the Assistant says you don't know how to run a really *big* farm; the Associate says you always miss the subtle, the very fine nuances, the minor behind-the-scenes details, and notice only the grossly obvious. Jack will feel better and bigger to overhear and deliver their comments; the Associate and Assistant will feel better for having flatulated their negative feelings. And none of them will know that Hal has decided the only thing left to do in regards to the secretary is to follow his original idea. He hopes to get her to quit voluntarily. After being seduced and spurned, why would she *want* to keep the job? He's sensitive and has it figured out: this is the only way she'll be able to leave feeling it was *her* decision to go, feeling righteous.

He can't get her to leave the outer-office, so he brings a cot. Hal's been told he's good in bed, but he's not afraid to try it with a cot. He gives it his best, which includes nipping, light pinching, long neck kisses, soft sucking, back and buttock massage, foot-licking, tongue-tickling, slurping, devouring, etcetera. The secretary added the *etcetera*: she's using shorthand. She notes the time of his climax and files it under inner-office memos. But she doesn't clean up his mess on the cot. Housekeeping isn't part of her job description.

Hal says, "That wasn't very good, it was a mistake, I don't want to do it again, *ever*, understand?"

Maybe the plan will work. She doesn't look at him. Because he's sensitive, Hal leaves so she can come to her decision and clean out her desk alone.

When Jack reports early in the morning, he has a typed document based on an in-depth observation of the Associate and Assistant farming directors, including an appendix in which he discusses the implications of various gestures and theorizes on the future of the farm based on these incidents, which are not isolated, he points out, but are becoming trends. Not only that, the Associate Director passed his job on to a hand who traded the six pregnant horses for eight geldings and thought he'd made an incredible deal. Meanwhile the Assistant Director is interviewing all his relatives and girlfriends for the vacant horse-breeding job.

Hal is stiff from having slept all night on the couch. His wife already knows about the cot incident, so now he'll have to find out who the snitch is. He looks at Jack's report. "Who typed this?" he wants to know.

"Who else?" Jack says. "When's her last day? I thought you were going to let her go."

Hal has only two choices. He can add *secretary* to the payroll list in the new budget request. Or he can stop being so sensitive.

The Something Bad

Early in the evening, when Crystal began chain-smoking, Hilary's already irritated right eye started to swell. The eye cried, so she plucked at the tissues Marta kept close because it was April and the pollen count was high.

Marta left the room to answer the phone. Neither Crystal nor Hilary said anything, the only motion Crystal's arm lifting her cigarette, Hilary's hand dabbing her eye. Then Marta said the phone call was for Crystal. Crystal shrieked, jumped over the back of the couch and ran into the kitchen. She was an old college pal of Marta's, visiting for a month. Hilary lived down the street. In twenty minutes the phone call was finished, Crystal was back, this time sitting on the floor, smoking one after another from her crumpled pack of cigarettes, in between hits on a bong which belonged to Marta's boyfriend who was out taking Marta's kids to their father for the weekend.

"Well ...?" Crystal said with a mouthful of smoke, either coming in or going out, "shall I tell you?"

"Tell us what?" Marta asked.

"That was Misty. She's seeing a therapist and just remembered or realized the other day ... a man I was married to for three years when she was very little ... he molested her ... no intercourse or anything, just when he would go to kiss her goodnight .... It was repressed, I guess, all this time. God, I could kill him. I really believed he was going in to say goodnight. I let him go alone. I could kill him."

"How is she?" Marta asked.

"Misty?" Crystal stared at the lit end of her cigarette. "She's fine. She's working it out. She was afraid to tell me, though. That gets me too. And this guy, he's married to someone else with young children now. I got a card at Christmas. I'll have to write to his new wife to warn her."

"Is that really what you should do?" Marta asked, reaching for a tissue. This was one of those nights she hadn't been able to taste and had left half her dinner on her plate at the restaurant they'd gone to earlier.

"You bet your ass I should!" Crystal rocked forward so she was on all fours, her face pushed forward toward Marta. Hilary, off to one side, saw their profiles, with Crystal leaning forward like a cornered dog. "Why shouldn't I, if I can keep him from doing it to someone else, what the fuck do you *mean* saying I shouldn't do it, how could I *not* do it!"

"But are you doing it for yourself, for your mother-guilt, or for the children?"

"You're damn right I have mother-guilt, what goddamn difference does it make why I do it as long as I keep him from touching someone else's kids. I should've protected my own daughter. But maybe I can stop him from hurting someone else."

"You're blaming yourself when you had absolutely nothing to do with it," Marta said.

Hilary looked from one to the other, tears streaming from her eye. "It's Misty's problem, not yours," she said. "And if she's handling it, what more can you do?"

"What do you know, you and your *dogs*," Crystal said, settling back against the couch. She lit the bong, sucking against it. The water sounded like a coffee pot.

"So," Marta said to Hilary, "has Will called you this week?"

"Of course not." Hilary listened to her own words, then was surprised, almost afraid. She touched her eye. "I mean, he's not going to call from home."

"Doesn't she ever go to the store or something?"

"He won't call anyway. He keeps it totally separate. He won't even think about calling."

"God, you're a fool," Crystal said.

"What right do I have to expect anything different?" Hilary pressed a tissue to her eye.

"*Right*? You've got the right to not be treated like a dirty comic book kept by a little boy under his mattress. Don't *you* think you're worth better treatment?"

"But if I ask for him to change, he'll leave me."

"Good, you'd be better off," Crystal said. "And anyway, he *has* left you."

"It's temporary. He'll be back."

"You've been dealing with it pretty well," Marta said.

"Sometimes," Hilary wasn't looking at ether of them while she talked, "I feel like his hand."

"Like his hand," Crystal snorted. "What the fuck does that mean?"

"It's something his hand does." But she couldn't explain, wouldn't describe out loud that while she touches him softly— grazes her fingertips on his sex, whirls gently around the head or uses a gathering-cotton motion with all five fingers barely skimming—his hand hovers nearby, like conducting music, wanting to brush aside the fly-light teasing touch and grab himself, but also not wanting to, so his hand beats time in the air, waiting, wondering when he (or it) will cave in, wondering what it wants: to continue the build-up or dive in and end it.

"He wondered," Hilary said, "what it would take to make me raise my voice, to make me mad, to make me shout at him or something. I said there would have to be something bad. I don't mind just that he doesn't call …. But if *I* say, I want to see you tonight ….Well, I feel like I *can't* say that. I wait and go crazy until *he* says it. I wonder if *this* is the something bad."

Crystal had stared at Hilary until she was finished. Then said, "This ain't it. It'll be worse." She used the bong again, then passed it to Marta. Hilary had a glass of wine. She dipped one finger in and patted the liquid on her swollen eye. She thought of saying, *But sometimes if I go crazy first, seeing him is better than ever—in fact, seeing him is never bad*, but didn't say it, not out loud. Her time with Will was full of want: he wanted to be there, she wanted him there, she wanted to be touched, he wanted to touch her. His watch that beeped once an hour sometimes beeped three or four times—sometimes she felt molded like soft wax, sometimes robust and wired, or graceful like an underwater dancer, or weightless in a warm vacuum; or panting, dry-mouthed and astonished that after three or four hours there were still only peaks, no valleys, and his voice coming from where his face was pressed to her neck or breast, thanking her for allowing him to touch her so long.

Crystal said, "This is it, women, this is mother-guilt. That's what this is, all right."

Marta crawled to where Crystal was sitting on the floor with her back against the couch. They hugged awkwardly, Marta on her knees with her arms around Crystal, leaning forward, falling into Crystal. Hilary stayed cross-legged on the floor in front of the chair, one eye crying.

"I was walking one of my dogs today," Hilary said, "and we passed a dog that had been hit by a car. It was lying dead on the sidewalk. My dog kept looking back, over her shoulder, after we passed it. Her expression was—Well, she's had puppies ... I think she was upset seeing something like that on the street."

"I think she smelled a dead animal," Crystal said.

"Maybe so ... but ...." She didn't want to explain the difference—how when they walked past a dead mouse or rat, the dog's head dove for it like a frog's tongue or a chicken stabbing at bugs, and she had to use a snap on the leash to jerk the dog away from the carrion before she got it into her mouth. Not having said that out loud, she also wasn't describing to them the next thing she thought about: the first time she'd lifted her head, slid her cheek down his chest and stomach, touched him with her tongue, took him gently between her lips, then all the way into her mouth, but he held her head and pulled her away. Why? she'd asked, afterwards or in the morning. He said something like, I'm afraid it's a degrading situation for you. It's not, she said, but didn't say: *it's powerful*. The next time he didn't pull her away so soon, and then stopped pulling her away at all. But still, just last week his hoarse voice and hot breath had panted into her ear, "Please, I *need* to know that you like to do that. I need to know."

Marta stretched out on her back in the middle of the floor. She held her temples with her fingertips. "Damn allergies. Anyway, I think he's really insensitive not to call."

"That's not why he doesn't ...," Hilary said. "But if I went away, I'd've probably—"

"Yes, *you* would," Crystal said. "Where's your self respect? This guy says you're good enough to give him a squirt in this armpit town, but outside of here you don't exist for him ... you don't exist when *he's* outside of here. Me, I'd tell him to go fuck himself."

"That's not exactly what it's like."

"Oh no? Look, this bastard I was married to when Misty was four. He said he *loved* her. And he supposedly loved me. What could he have meant? He was molesting my daughter, my baby, for Christ's sake, a baby!"

"Men mean a different thing," Marta said. "The L word is different."

"Yes, it's different." Hilary's voice was almost a whisper. Her eye throbbed.

"You brought this on yourself," Crystal said.

"I know." Marta and Hilary said it simultaneously, then looked at each other, Marta still on her back on the floor. Marta laughed, covering her eyes and cheeks with her hands again. "Oh my sinuses .... We called off the wedding, you know."

Crystal worked the bong. The water spit inside it.

"We decided together, we talked about it," Marta said. "It felt like we were, I don't know, rushing to finish something, having to hurry and make plans, rearranging everything to fit something in just because we somehow got the idea that's when it *had* to be. But also ...." She took the bong from Crystal but didn't pick up the lighter. She held the bong on her stomach, looking up at the ceiling.

Hilary's right eye was almost completely swollen shut. Water still oozed from between the lids.

"He hasn't lived his own life yet," Marta said. "He's adopting my life, my friends, my kids. Why is that so scary to me?"

"It should be scary to him," Hilary said.

"That's right!" Marta put the bong on the rug beside her and touched her temples again, then ran her fingers around her eyes.

"None of my husbands was like that," Crystal said. "Just hippies and bums. And a child molester. Oh, Misty, be strong, girl. I'm sorry, I'm sorry." Crystal threw her head back onto the seat of the couch. Hilary pulled her legs toward her chest and put her forehead on her knees. There was no music. A Moody Blues tape had ended just before Crystal's phone call. The amplifier was still on, the speakers still breathing slightly. Hilary thought of telling Marta the speakers were live (the amp burning out maybe) but didn't want to have to explain that she often lay awake and listened to Will breathing in his sleep— deep, slow, open breathing, pure rest, although he apologized for snoring, wondered how she put up with it. His sleeping breath changed to a softly moaned "Ohhh" when she pressed against him or passed her hand down his back.

"So Will's coming back day after tomorrow?" Marta said. "What's he do here, anyway?"

"The phone company is having him here, six weeks on, a week off, for six months. To set up some systems at various places."

"We're some jungle in Africa and he's the missionary sent to bring civilization," Crystal said.

"He's got two months left." Hilary looked up.

"And after that?" Marta asked.

"He goes home. They reassign him to trouble-shoot somewhere else."

"Where he shoots *into* some*one* else, right?" Crystal said.

"I don't know if that's true."

"Because what would it *mean* if it were!" Crystal's head snapped upright again. "Is being alone really worse?"

"Peter's afraid of being alone, I think," Marta said. "But anyone who's been through a divorce already knows ...."

Crystal lit another cigarette, dragged on it, put it in her ashtray then leaned forward to take the bong back. After she hit on the bong, she said, "Give Marta a face massage. You can do that, can't you?"

On her knees, Hilary edged over beside Marta and began to run her fingertips across Marta's forehead, down her cheeks, under her eyes. She looked up once. Crystal was watching with an acute stare. Hilary didn't notice how dim the room was until Crystal's voice seemed to come out of darkness, as though from a far corner of the room, "Misty couldn't ask to be treated with dignity and respect, but I'm her mother, I should've made *damn* sure she was."

Barely out loud, Hilary said, "Who's going to make sure for us now?"

Crystal made a sharp sound in her throat. Hilary didn't say anything about the several times Will had murmured, "I can't believe the things you let me do to you." Once was the morning after he'd awakened her at 3 a.m., his hand sliding down her bare backside—without acknowledging that she was no longer sleeping, she'd raised her butt as his fingers slipped between her legs. She also didn't tell *him*, not at the time and the appropriate moment never returned, that it wasn't a matter of *letting him*, it was a matter of *want*.

From under Hilary's fingers, Marta said, "Remember when we went out on New Year's, the year of my divorce ... you spent the whole time dancing with Johnny ...."

"My *husband*," Crystal said. "Is that a crime?"

"I cried in the bathroom."

"*My* fault?"

Hilary continued to trace the outline of Marta's face, swirled circles across her forehead, on her temples, used her thumbs on her cheeks, ran a finger down the bridge of her nose. Marta said, "I just couldn't even tell if it was you or Johnny I wanted attention from."

Hilary's fingers stopped. Then she brushed Marta's hair from her brow and back away from her ears, thought of saying, but didn't, that for some reason, because of Will, she could even touch herself with more sincerity, like the way she touched him ... or anyone else. He'd wanted her to tell him a secret, and during her secret his finger moved in and out of her. She told him about the early times when he'd been coming to her building to evaluate the business phone system, and one day he was giving a demo and she watched his hands pushing buttons on the equipment, then suddenly she had to back up and sink into her chair, let the demo go on as she receded, because she was picturing him, his hand, with her.

"Now you tell a secret," she'd said, and he told his, but without his finger inside her. He held her hand, and their hands rested together on her stomach, at first. His voice was a throaty whisper, the sentences broken, she couldn't've— with all the grass or wine in the world—duplicated for Crystal and Marta what he said against her ear, their joined hands slightly moving, together, on her body. *I was living with a woman— It was nighttime— We were stoned— sitting in the living room on the couch— She had a Franklin stove— We could see the flames in it— It was across from the couch— We were just sitting there— We were pretty stoned— She had her shirt up or off— I got up to go to bed— I was in the bedroom— This was the way things usually happened— Get up and go to bed— Was taking off my clothes— Something wasn't right— She hadn't followed me into the bedroom— It seemed unusual— because I was stoned— otherwise I might've just called her name— But I went back out there— She didn't know I was there— Her jeans were pushed down— Her eyes were closed— Her hands were in her underwear— She knew exactly how to touch herself— Her fingers knew— how to make her body feel— She was moving, giving herself— so much pleasure— It was— just so— pretty—*

Someone sighed. Hilary began to touch Marta's face with only one hand and held her own swollen eye with her other hand. She cried into her palm. Crystal was massaging Marta's feet. "You guys," Marta said weakly. Hilary put her brow against Marta's stomach, felt Marta's muscles tighten, lifted her head quickly again, looked at Marta—her eyes were closed—looked at Crystal, holding Marta's feet. Crystal met Hilary's eyes without a flicker. She slowly lowered her face again to Marta's body.

Someone put a foot under Hilary's shoulder and rolled her over, away from Marta. It was Crystal, standing up, dressed in a robe and slippers. A damp washcloth, folded neatly, lay across Marta's eyes and nose. Crystal said, "You'd better leave here."

"Why?"

"Marta has more important problems. So do I."

"What should I do?" Hilary asked, pulling herself upright, propping herself against the couch. She reached for her shirt.

"Do? Go take care of your dogs. I don't give a shit."

Marta moaned softly.

"Go wait," Crystal said, "for your precious *Will* ... who *won't* call and *won't* remember you after he leaves here for good."

"Yes he will."

Crystal was almost turned away, then whirled back and swung at Hilary with both fists, hitting her first on one ear, then the other.

"Dirty fucking *dyke*, get the hell out of here!"

Hilary put her pants on, found her shoes and socks, buttoned her shirt without looking up. She walked carefully around Marta, heard Crystal's feet thumping behind her—she flinched, ducking her head a little, but Crystal's footsteps went into the kitchen. It was early Sunday morning. She knew what she would find at home: the happy wagging faces of her dogs behind their kennel gates. And a light on her phone machine that hadn't started blinking green. Her eye was puffed out, cemented shut. She couldn't tell how far away the front door was. She would call Marta later and apologize vaguely. But she would never tell them about the night before Will left: At some point, in darkness, she had said, "Am I allowed to say I'll miss you?"

"No," he'd said, "don't say that. Don't give me a second thought."

He had stayed behind her, she can't remember when she last saw his face. They moved all over his small apartment, from dark corners into a fluorescent kitchen, from the hot bathroom to the living room (kneeling, her face on the sofa), to the bedroom in front of the mirror, but there was no light there and her head was thrown back—she'd seen no reflection. Held upright against him, lifted off her feet, he spun and took her along, as though pivoting on his heels, then they were falling backwards onto the bed, rolling over, his weight covered her for only a few minutes. And he'd hardly spoken. And she could barely understand him when he did. He either whispered, *It all hardly seems real, does it?* or *You'll always feel it*, or something else entirely. By the time they were back in the living room again, her forehead against the front door, his body still pressed behind her, he did say, clearly, "Please tell me if you don't like something I'm doing, if anything's bad for you. I'm afraid I'm going to break you!"

"I'm not that fragile," she'd gasped.

"Good."

They stayed collapsed against the door another ten minutes ... or twenty minutes ... or two hours .... He pulled up her pants, buttoned her blouse. She leaned back against him and watched his hand, as though it was hers, reaching out to open the door in front of her, just wide enough for her to leave. So she had left. And drove home. And had turned around to close her own door behind herself, but her knees buckled. The first time it had been a mistake—her head just fell against the door. After that she had jammed the doorknob into her eye five times before she stopped.

Hesitation

It's not that he left after fucking her because he wanted to get away from her. It's not that he wouldn't've enjoyed the heat of her beside him or her hand creeping inside his underwear in the morning when they would both be groggy and he was hard but not urgent. He would've liked her to hold it while he slept. But what if he were with her and the phone rang at 1 or 2 in the morning, and what if it were his ex-wife calling? Once he lay spread eagle and said, Tie me up and do whatever you want to me. She actually put her tongue in his armpit, sucked his toes, rubbed his hard-on between her breasts. The jewel in her pierced nose scratched gently on his stomach as she nipped and licked around his navel, growling like a puppy, laughed and said she was eating away the cord he'd forgotten to cut. So she can't piss her poison into you no more, the girl said, it's not like she's your fuckin' *mother*. It's not that he still went out with his ex-wife because he liked her company. It's just that he'd destroyed someone's whole world and he owed that much in return, so she wouldn't feel like a worthless person, so she wouldn't feel totally abandoned. More than once he wet the girl's neck with his tears. She touched his cheeks and kissed his face and sometimes he held her hard, but the worst time he just stared at the ceiling through his brimming eyes because the woman had said he was selfish and always got what he wanted but never wanted to take care of her and never wanted to give her what she wanted and he was always constantly shoving that thing at her but why didn't he hold her hand or take her to hear the symphony play outside at the waterfront at night—so why should she want to have sex with him?—and now he's ruined her plan for her life because they were supposed to grow old together in their lovely home and now she'll be alone and even though she was going on a vacation cruise to the Mediterranean next week, think how awful it would be for her knowing he'd be with that weirdo filthy girl, doing whatever he wants, how was that supposed to make her feel? It would ruin her trip, she said. It's not that he thought the woman had actually guessed his reverie that the girl helped bring to life as soon as the Rome-bound jet was off the ground: a hungry, vibrant creature wearing an evening gown slit up the back to her bare ass who wandered around among the crowd at the opera until she chose him out of a whole theater full of people and followed him to the downtown pier, begging him to fuck her on the rail above angry, violent breakers lapping at the pylons 100 feet from shore as embarrassed tourists hurried past in salty milk-warm darkness, pretending not to notice. It's not that he felt guilty or wrong for making love to the girl like that, after all those years of his own spit. It's not like he vacillated at all, it's not as though he'd had any qualms, that he wasn't flying on adrenalin as he and the girl made up those fantasies while eating take-out ribs in the living room in their underwear and promised them to each other as gifts. It's not as though he wasn't absolutely exhilarated when she rolled him over and used colored pens to draw a tattoo on his butt. He saw it in the mirror later, a heart all wrung up like a dish cloth, with blood dripping out, a little smeared because she'd pressed her face over it before the ink was dry. She said, You mean none of those friends of yours ever said you've got a sexy ass? I'm gonna ask them why. It's not that he was reluctant to introduce her to his friends because he was ashamed of her. It's not that he thought they wouldn't like her, wouldn't think she's smart enough or sophisticated enough for him. He said after 20 years of knowing him with his wife, they weren't ready for him to appear suddenly with a new girl. They'd be uncomfortable. He wouldn't want to do that to them. He said maybe they always thought if their kids turned out like her, they'd feel like complete failures or kill themselves. Yeah, she said softly. He just meant he had to prepare them first. He couldn't imagine what they would think if he dropped in or showed up at a party unannounced with her. The girl suggested, maybe they'll wonder: wow, what's *he* got that *I* don't got? Maybe she didn't understand when he said don't ever tell anyone that another girl once fell in love with her. And don't ever tell anyone that a former lover took polaroid snapshots of her during foreplay before he beat her up. Don't talk about the head shop in Ocean Beach where she used to work, her alcoholic mother who held her down and shaved her head long before that style became popular, or why she was kicked out of bartender school. And don't show them her wrists where the scars stand up, cherry red, shiny just-born skin that sometimes she ran her tongue along while watching his collection of Bogart movies. Don't laugh and tell anyone they're called hesitation marks. Don't say it was the first new skin of a whole new girl, that there's a chart in some hospital basement saying 26 sutures, lacerations on right and left forearms, suicide gesture suspected. Don't mention at a dinner party that blood tastes like silver, if silver had a taste, that's what it would taste like—like blood. Don't talk about incest or abortions or hitchhiking or sugar-daddies or bull-dykes or body art or dildos. He only warned her because they would've wondered about her, would've thought funny thoughts about her, and he wanted them to know her as he knew her. He says in her case maybe first impressions wouldn't've told the whole story. It's not that he asked her not to wear sleeveless shirts in public because he didn't think her tattoos were cute. And it's not that he was wavering, the night he'd sent her home, as usual, but she crouched in the bushes outside his bedroom until dawn because she'd moved again and couldn't remember where she lived. If he'd known it was her he wouldn't've called the police. It's not that he doesn't care enough to call someone now, but how could he describe her to the police? He doesn't have a photograph of her to put up on telephone poles, and, even though he's not embarrassed of her fantasy, he wouldn't want to show them the videotape of it: the dark room with dozens of candles, the 24-hour road race from Le Mans on the television, him on the floor in jeans and bare feet, eating anchovy pizza and drinking 7-up from a can, the girl arriving like a thief through the glass slider behind the sofa, wearing crotch-length mini and spike heels with ankle straps, nothing underneath, and completely shaved, kisses his neck and ears but his eyes never move from the TV screen, he continues sipping the 7-up as she unbuttons his jeans, but not the top button, takes his cock and balls out of the fly, strokes him and licks the cheese from his fingertips as he finishes the soda and settles back against the sofa, leans sideways to see the TV, doesn't even close his eyes as she sucks his cock, but his toes curl and uncurl, then she straddles him, slides her shaved pussy right down over him, but the end of the fantasy was ruined—the part where the cars go into their final lap and he gets up, bends her onto her knees and fucks her from the rear—because a door opens in the background and someone says *Yoo-hoo,* and the woman he'd been married to comes into the picture, and there's absolutely no pause before the girl falls sideways, almost onto the candles, as he struggles to his feet to hurry after the woman who has run from the room. The video camera kept filming until the tape was finished. He doesn't reappear in the picture, but it does show the girl leaving through the slider, splashing through the glass like water. He used to tell the girl he needed her. He used to talk about how she was the only one he could turn to, the only one on his side. He used to say no one else had ever given him as much as she did. Once he'd told her she was a dream come true. Once he said she'd saved his life.

Former Virgin

When I heard this story a few weeks ago, I wished I could tell you about it. I don't know why. A guy named Roger told me the story about himself and someone named Wanda, but I didn't tell him about you. He might've asked why I don't see you anymore, and what could I have said, that I cried too much? I don't really know why. Do I?

If I *had* mentioned you to Roger, I would've had to tell him that you and I weren't the same as him and me. You knew me a different way. Didn't you? There's a way I could've explained it: Remember the time your wife gave me some of her old clothes? At first I was afraid to wear them, but when I finally came to work in one of the dresses, you said, "I recognize that dress," because no one else would know what you were talking about, so it was okay to say it. You smiled a funny way every time I wore one of them. I still have those dresses, and I still wear them, but no one recognizes them anymore.

Roger wouldn't've understood but it doesn't matter because I only saw him that one time. How would you look, I wonder, if I told you he and I were having this conversation in bed. But I won't try to imagine it. I wouldn't want you to know.

Maybe the only true similarity is that Roger was Wanda's teacher just like you were my boss. He was her graduate advisor. I don't know what he advised her in. He read her poems, analyzed her paintings, critiqued her plays, studied her clothing designs, discussed her photography technique, suggested good books and movies, played her songs on his piano. And he started calling her and visiting her in her windy one-room apartment where she served herb tea that tasted like dirt or perfume, and dried figs and humus and pita bread. (Her bed was behind a curtain in the corner.) She had shaved her head a few months before and her hair was a soft one-inch long, making her tiny ears stick out a little. One of her dresses was a black parachute flak jacket. She also had a pair of tight black peg-leg jeans which she usually wore with a size-large V-neck man's undershirt. She put the V around in back. She wore her sweaters that way too. Once she showed Roger a pretty gray pull-over she said she'd bought when she was accepted into graduate school and knew she had to be more dressed up. Then she always wore it inside-out with the V neck in back and the label in front, under her chin.

"Too bad the label didn't say 100% virgin wool," I said to Roger, but I wouldn't want you to hear me say something like that, lying there naked in bed. You'll never know this about me.

But she was no virgin—it was too late for that. Not that it matters. Not that anyone is anymore.

Several times in the few weeks since I saw Roger, I've imagined telling you his story about Wanda, but I can't picture where we'd be. I couldn't have told you at work. You'd know why: In your office I told you things like my credit application was rejected and my car was dented while sitting innocently alone in a parking lot. I like to remember how you smiled and said, "Credit is easy, Cleo," and helped me make a new application. "Once you're credible, you'll wish you weren't." And you said the dent in my car would be a good reminder for me—that's what I deserve for allowing my car to remain innocent so long. But to tell you Roger's story, I would've had to shut the door, and it was a good policy, you said, that we never do that. Lunch was also not a good time for us to talk. Remember, I never said much at lunch. We used to go out with several other people and all sit together at a long booth where you would look at me from the corner of your eye, or across the table, and smile once or twice, or say something about someone else that only I would understand.

Of course there was that time I was at your house, but we had something else to talk about that day.

Most of Roger's story starts when Wanda came to his office after a seminar. She had left class early and he thought she'd come back to ask what had happened during the second hour and to find out when they were going to see the new Italian movie at the Guild. It was spring and had rained that day, so she had her black rubber boots and oiled parasol, and a black leather jacket over her white undershirt. He said her hair looked soft, like the fur on a little brown laboratory mouse. But her eyes, he said— he could never remember how her eyes looked, even a minute after she walked out of a room.

She sat as usual in the chair beside his desk and pulled her notebook out of her leather book bag. There was nothing held in the rings of the notebook, but between the covers she kept a yellow legal pad. She folded the pages over when they were full of writing, until the first ones got weak and came loose, so she had to fold them in half and put them between pages of her books. She also dug around in her bag for a pen, then tested it on the yellow paper. Tested it over and over, making curly-cue lines down both sides and across the top and bottom. She began coloring in the loops and said, "That woman who sits at the end of the table is really hostile, don't you think so, Roger? I'm sure she thinks I'm a spoiled little rich girl."

"What makes you think so?" Roger said.

"She's always late to class and never says anything. Or she sighs or says *hmmmm* or *Oh!*"

"That's a revealing perception." At this point Roger smiled while telling the story, and he brushed some hair out of my eyes which made my stomach kink-up and burn like hunger.

"Yes," Wanda said. "Do you think everyone has the wrong idea about us? The man across from me doesn't think I have anything important to say. He thinks I'm just trying to discredit him to make myself look better."

"Oh really?"

"Don't you see the way he looks at me over the top of his glasses—without raising his head—and he stirs his coffee while I'm talking, or spills it. When I tried to clean it up for him once, he said, *forget it—go on with what you were trying to say.* Do you remember that?"

Roger asked, "Is there some problem, Wanda?"

She seemed a little surprised and sat back in her chair, looking at him. He didn't even remember if she wore glasses or not. He said she had a very dainty chin and wide cheekbones. Her eyes may've been brown or green, he said. He'd been trying to remember. But *I* don't have any problem remembering: on your balcony, it was dusk, and as the sun set your eyes changed from blue to violet.

"Well," Wanda said in her same unsurprised soft voice, "I've been feeling uncomfortably anxious in class to the point where I don't feel I can sit there any more. I'm a distraction and it makes me nervous."

"This is absolutely lucid, Wanda," he said.

"What do you mean?" She cocked her head, only slightly.

"Well, you can't stand the thought that everyone might be paying undue attention to you, so you stand and leave the room, which causes everyone to stare after you."

"I didn't mean to disrupt the class."

"But isn't that why you left?"

"Certainly not!" She stopped doodling on her paper.

"I'm not chastising you, Wanda," Roger said. "I'm trying to help."

"I don't want our relationship to be based on you helping me." She still held her pen with both hands in her lap, twisting and turning it between her fingers, unscrewing it, fiddling with the insides, then screwing it back together.

"Do I make you nervous in class, Wanda?"

Again she was speechless for a second, but her hands didn't stop. She looked down at what she was doing to her pen. "I think," she said, her voice even higher and softer, "I shouldn't have chosen to sit so close to you."

Then after a moment Roger got up and shut the door of his office. When he turned around again, Wanda was standing behind him, and they embraced.

He said he heard the rain outside. Otherwise the room was silent. He seemed to have a difficult time telling me this part. He thought for a long moment, and I heard my clock humming, and right then as we lay in bed, I almost told him what I was thinking about: That evening, when you stood and went to the balcony rail, I rubbed my eyes and wiped my nose on my sleeve. The heavy air was salty. I heard you say "Maybe there won't be a fog tonight," and when I could see again, I stared at your glass of red wine balancing on the rail.

They went to her place. Did I forget to mention that Roger was married? It doesn't make any difference; he and his wife had separate bedrooms. He found out that under Wanda's black jeans she wore black silk underwear, but under her white T-shirt she wore a simple white cotton bra. Then I think he felt a little embarrassed, talking about their sex while lying in bed with me. He stroked my back and down over my rump. I told him it was okay. It makes me glad I'll never see you again.

When they were finished, Roger wanted to talk and Wanda wanted to go out. "Let's do both," she said. She got out clean black underwear and a clean white bra, but put on the same black jeans and white undershirt, then the black jacket and black boots. She stood at the door with her green parasol, jingling her keys in one hand.

She picked the restaurant. He said it was called Earth's Own Garden, and a whole side of the menu was dedicated to herb healing. "Nothing real happens in a vegetarian restaurant," he said to her, and she laughed. Her laugh, he said, was like a music box.

After they ordered he told her about his only other experience with a vegetarian restaurant. Someone was leaving the faculty and they were having a farewell dinner for him. Since he was a vegetarian, they chose a vegetarian restaurant. They were all supposed to meet there, but Roger had an afternoon class which ran later than usual that day, so he decided it wouldn't be worth it to go to the dinner at all. He called the place and asked them to page the party from the university. "I'm sorry," the hostess answered, "this is a vegetarian restaurant— we don't page our customers."

Wanda ordered the smallest salad and sat eating the alfalfa sprouts with her fingers, one at a time. He smiled and said, "What color are your eyes?" She stared at him and he still didn't know.

"You don't seem changed by this," he said.

"Were you hoping I would be?"

"I know *I* am."

"No you're not." She stirred her salad, looking for more sprouts.

He tried smiling again. "Well, it was a first for me—first time on a couch."

She found a sprout and ate it in three bites.

"Next time let's use the bed, okay?" he said.

"I don't like people to see my bedroom."

Roger ordered coffee. "We have grain beverages and herb tea," the waitress said.

"Don't you have anything dangerously flavorful?" Roger joked with her. She had thin brown lips. Wanda wore red lipstick when she went out, but her lips were pretty and pale when, before this had happened to them, he used to drop in to see her, unexpected, on Saturdays.

"I know what," Wanda said brightly. "Let's go to the theater on B street. They have a French movie. We can talk without disturbing anyone because they'll be reading the subtitles."

"We could go back to your place."

She was already standing, putting on her leather jacket. She turned, her hands in her jacket pockets. He said she looked like a young lovely punk.

"The heat's not working in my building," she said. "Didn't you notice?"

I wasn't chilly on your balcony until the sun was gone and a wind jumped out of the ocean. I rubbed the bumps on my arms. You never shivered. Your hands were steady as you looked through the telescope mounted on the balcony rail.

The movie had already started. Wanda leaned toward Roger to see the screen between the two heads in front of her. "Wanda, we do have to talk," Roger said. She was holding her wallet in both hands in her lap as she always did in the movies. "I don't want you to misunderstand," he said.

"You mean about our affair?" she said.

"I don't like that word. It doesn't have to be like that— cheap, secret."

Then Roger looked a little embarrassed again and stopped talking, even bent over to give my shoulder a sad kiss.

"It's okay," I told him. "I know there's a difference between her and me."

"Thank you," he said, touching my face again.

Wanda sighed and said, "Wonderful." She was looking at the screen, a wet black-and-white view of Paris.

"Wanda." He put his hand on her arm and saw that her fingers tightened on her wallet. But she did turn to face him. "Something important is happening to us," he said.

"Do you really think so?" she said.

"I want to know what *you* think."

"I'm flattered ... aren't you?"

"I just told you it's more than that."

Then Wanda said, "Oh!" and turned to read some dialogue on the screen.

Why wouldn't you stop looking through that telescope? There were no stars. The sky a rose-colored gray. I still remember everything. You knew I would.

"What's happening?" Roger whispered.

"Nothing yet."

"I mean to us."

She didn't answer. Her red lips parted. Her eyes moved across the lines of dialogue.

"I'm going," Roger said out loud. "I hope that you'll meet me outside."

She did come out, and she was smiling at him. She put her wallet in the pocket of her leather jacket and took his arm. But he didn't start walking with her. "Look," he said, "we have to make some things clear."

You never said anything like that. Maybe there was some fog after all, moving inland. "Pull yourself together, Cleo." You finally turned around, but stayed at the rail. "I think you want to look at the world through a Vaseline-covered lens." No lights on the balcony, but I could see your mouth moving.

"It's already clear to me," Wanda said, and she pulled so hard on his arm that Roger had to start walking with her.

"Then tell me how you see us." He said it was the same way they discussed her stories and plays: he told her nothing was happening and she said it was. But this was backwards.

Then she stopped outside a newsstand. "I catch my bus on the next corner, Roger," she said. She gave him a swift kiss on the cheek. "I'll be all right. I have to pick up something here. Drive carefully, it may rain again."

"Wait a minute!" She had already started to go into the newsstand, but he pulled her back. "I know you, Wanda—you starved yourself on grass for supper and now you don't want me to know that you're going to go get yourself some candy bars to eat on the bus!"

"Roger!" she gasped.

After a moment of staring at each other, he said, "It's okay, Wanda," and he touched her face. I shivered. He wasn't touching me then. He was lying on his back talking to the ceiling. He said he didn't remember what she looked like as she listened. His words came out slowly, his voice low, hard to understand.

"Wanda, dear," he said to her, "maybe you can't face the world without your alfalfa sprouts ... it's okay. I'd just like to be closer to you than anyone else has been—to be allowed to see you eat, sleep, maybe even cry once in a while." He *wanted* to see her cry. What does it mean?

Did he stop mumbling or did I stop listening? We lay there a while, then he said, "And you can guess what happened next, otherwise I wouldn't be here with you—Oh, I'm sorry."

"It's okay."

After a while I said to Roger, "How about if, after nailing you, someone told you you're not the center of the universe to anyone but yourself," even though you looked at me and smiled, your words spoken so softly, and the background was a dying day. You may remember what I looked like, but it's not how I look anymore.

Roger didn't say anything else. I think he left soon after that. I stayed there in bed for a long time. But only virgins cry.

NB 10/97